THE CAMP FIRE GIRLS AT CAMP KEEWAYDIN

or

Down Paddles

HILDEGARD G. FREY

1st WORLD
LIBRARY
Literary Society

The Campfire Girls at Camp Keewaydin

Hildegard G. Frey

© 1st World Library – Literary Society, 2005
PO Box 2211
Fairfield, IA 52556
www.1stworldlibrary.org
First Edition

LCCN: 2006930811

Softcover ISBN: 1-4218-2185-0
Hardcover ISBN: 1-4218-2085-4
eBook ISBN: 1-4218-2285-7

Purchase *"The Campfire Girls at Camp Keewaydin"*
as a traditional bound book at:
www.1stWorldLibrary.org/purchase.asp?ISBN=1-4218-2185-0

1st World Library Literary Society is a nonprofit
organization dedicated to promoting literacy by:

- Creating a free internet library accessible from any
  computer worldwide.
- Hosting writing competitions and offering book
  publishing scholarships.

The Campfire Girls at Camp Keewaydin
contributed by Tim, Ed & Rodney
in support of
1st World Library Literary Society

CHAPTER I

ON THE WAY

"All aboard!" The hoarse voice of Captain MacLaren boomed out like a fog horn, waking a clatter of echoes among the tall cliffs on the opposite shore of the river, and sending the seventy-five girls on the dock all skurrying for the *Carribou's* gangplank at once.

"Hurry up, Hinpoha! We're getting left behind." Agony strained forward on the suitcase she was helping Hinpoha to carry down the hill and endeavored to catch up with the crowd, a proceeding which she soon acknowledged to be impossible, for Hinpoha, rendered breathless by the hasty scramble from the train, lagged farther behind with every step.

"I - can't - go - any - faster!" she panted, and abruptly let go of her end of the suitcase to fan herself with her hand. "What's the use of rushing so, anyway?" she demanded plaintively. "They won't go off without us; they can see us coming down the hill. It wasn't *my* fault that my camera got wedged under the seat and made us be the last ones off the train," she continued, "and I'm not going to run down this hill and go sprawling, like I did in the elevator yesterday. Are the other girls on already?" she asked, searching the crowd below with her eyes for a sight of the other Winnebagos.

"Sahwah and Oh-Pshaw are on the boat already," replied Agony, "and Gladys and Migwan are just getting on. I don't see Katherine anywhere, however. Oh, yes," she exclaimed, "there she is down there in the crowd. What are they all laughing at, I wonder? Oh, look, Katherine's suitcase has come open, and all her things are spilled out on the dock. I thought it would be strange if she made the trip without some kind of a mishap. Oh, dear, did you ever see anyone so funny as Katherine?"

"Well," observed Hinpoha in a tone of relief, "we don't have to hurry now. It'll take them at least ten minutes to get that suitcase shut again. I know, because I helped Katherine pack. I had to sit on it with all my might to close it."

"*All Aboard!*" came the second warning roar from Captain MacLaren, accompanied by a deafening blast of the *Carribou's* whistle. Agony picked up Hinpoha's suitcase in one hand and her own in the other, and with an urgent "Come on!" made a dash down the remainder of the hill and landed breathless at the gangplank of the waiting steamer just as the engine began to quiver into motion. Hinpoha was just behind her, and Katherine trod closely upon Hinpoha's heels, carrying her still unclosed suitcase out before her like a tray, to keep its contents from spilling out.

Migwan was waiting for them at the head of the gangplank. "We've saved a place for you up in the bow," she said. "Hurry up, we're having *such* a time holding it for you. The boat is simply *packed.*"

The four girls picked their way through a litter of suitcases, paddles, cameras, tennis rackets and musical instruments that covered every inch of deck space between the chairs, and joined the other Winnebagos in their place in the bow. Hinpoha sank down gratefully upon a deck chair that Oh-Pshaw had obligingly been holding for her and Agony disposed herself upon a pile of suitcases, from which vantage point she could get a good look at the crowd.

The *Carribou* had turned her nose about and was gliding

Hildegard G. Frey

smoothly upstream, following the random curvings of the lazy Onawanda as it wound through the low-lying, wooded hills of the Shenandawah country, singing a carefree wanderer's song as it flowed. It was a glorious, balmy day in late June, dazzlingly blue and white, sparklingly golden. It was the *Carribou's* big day of the year, that last day of June. On all other days she made her run demurely from Lower Falls Station to Upper Falls, carrying freight and a handful of passengers on each trip; but every year on that last day of June freight and ordinary passengers stood aside, for the *Carribou* was chartered to carry the girls of Camp Keewaydin to their summer hunting grounds.

The Winnebagos looked around with interest at the girls who were to be their companions for the summer, all as yet total strangers to them. Girls of every shape and size, of every shade of complexion, of every age between sixteen and twenty. A number were apparently "old girls," who had been at Camp Keewaydin in former years; they flocked together in the bow right behind the Winnebagos, chattering animatedly, singing snatches of camp songs, and uttering conjectures in regard to such things as whether they would be in the Alley or the Avenue; and who was going to be councilor in All Saints this year.

A number of these old girls were grouped in an adoring attitude around a pretty young woman who talked constantly in an animated tone, and at intervals strummed on a ukulele. Continual cries of "Pom-pom!" rose on the air from the circle surrounding her. It was "*Dear* Pom-pom," "Pom-pom, you angel," "O *darling* Pom-pom! Can't you fix it so that I can be in your tent this year?" and much more in the same strain.

"Pom-pom is holding her court again this year, I see," said a biting voice just behind Agony.

Agony maneuvered herself around on her perch and glanced down at the speaker. She was a decidedly plain girl with a thick nose and a wide mouth set in a grim line above an extraordinarily heavy chin. Her face was turned partly away as she spoke to the girl next to her, but Agony caught a glimpse of the sarcastic expression which informed her features, and a little chill of dislike went through her. Agony was extremely susceptible to first impressions of people.

The girl addressed made an inaudible reply and the first girl continued in low but emphatic tones, "Well, you won't catch me fetching and carrying for her and playing the part of the adoring slave, I can tell you. I think it's perfectly silly, the way the girls all get a crush on her."

There was a pause, and then the other girl asked, somewhat hastily, "Who do you suppose will get the Buffalo Robe this year?"

"Oh, Mary Sylvester will, of course," came the reply. "She nearly got it last year. Now that Peggy Atterbury isn't coming back Mary'll be the most popular girl in camp without a doubt. Look at her over there, trying to be sweet to Pompom."

"Isn't she stunning in that coral silk sweater?" murmured the other girl.

"She has too much color to wear that shade of pink," returned the sarcastic one.

Agony's eyes traveled over to the group surrounding Pom-pom and rested upon the girl who, next to Pom-pom herself, was the center of the group. She was very much like Agony herself, with intensely black hair, snow white forehead and richly red lips, though a little slighter in build and somewhat taller. A frank friendliness beamed from her clear dark eyes and her smile was warm and sincere. Agony felt drawn to her and jealous of her at the same time. *The most popular girl in camp.* That was the title Agony coveted with all her soul. To be prominent; to be popular, was Agony's chief aim in life; and to be pointed out in a crowd as *the* most popular girl seemed the one thing in the world most desirable to her. She, too, would be prominent and popular, she resolved; she, too, would be pointed out in the crowd.

The sarcastic voice again broke in upon her reverie. "Have you seen the hippopotamus over there in the bow? I should think a girl would be ashamed to get that stout."

Agony glanced apprehensively at Hinpoha, who was staring straight out over the water, but whose crimson face betrayed only too plainly that she had heard the remark. The rest of the Winnebagos had undoubtedly heard it also, as well as a number of others rubbing elbows with them, for a sudden embarrassed silence fell over that corner of the boat and a dozen pairs of eyes glanced from Hinpoha to the speaker, who, not one whit abashed, continued to stare scornfully at the object of her ridicule.

"Of all the bad manners!" said Agony to Sahwah in an indignant undertone, which, with the characteristic penetrating quality of Agony's voice, carried perfectly to the ears of the girl behind her. A light, satirical laugh was the reply. Agony turned to bestow a withering glance upon this rude creature, and met a pair of greenish tan eyes bent upon her with an expression of cool mockery. In the instant that their eyes met there sprang up between them one of those sudden antagonisms that are characteristic of very positive natures; the two hated each other cordially at first sight, before they had ever spoken a word to each other. Like fencers' swords their glances crossed and fell apart, and each girl turned her back pointedly upon the other. Broken threads of conversation were picked up by the group around them, shouts of laughter came from the group surrounding Pom-pom, who was reciting a funny poem, and the tense moment passed.

The other Winnebagos forgot the incident and gave themselves over to enjoyment of the beautiful scene which was unrolling before their eyes as the *Carribou* bore them further and further into the wilds; great dark stretches of woodland brooding in silence on the hillsides; an occasional glimpse of a far distant mountain peak wreathed in mist, and near by many a merry little stream romping down a hillside into the mother arms of the Onawanda. Gradually the shores had drawn close together until the travelers could look into the cool depths of the forests past which they were gliding, and could hear the calling of the wild birds in their leafy sanctuary.

Just past a long stretch of woods which Hinpoha thought might be enchanted, because the trees stood so stiffly straight, the *Carribou* rounded a bend, and there flashed into sight an irregular row of white tents scattered among the pines on a rise of ground some hundred or more feet back from the river.

"There's camp," Sahwah tried to say to Hinpoha, but her voice was drowned in the shriek of ecstasy which rose from the old campers. Handkerchiefs waved wildly; paddles smote the deck with deafening thumps; cheer after cheer rolled up, accompanied by the loud tooting of the *Carribou's* whistle. Captain MacLaren always joined in the racket of arrival as heartily as the girls themselves, taking delight in seeing how much noise he could coax from the throat of his steam siren.

Amid the racket the little vessel nosed her way up alongside a wooden dock, and before she was fairly fast the younger members of last year's delegation had leapt over the rail and were scurrying up the path. The older ones followed more sedately, having stopped to pick up their luggage, and to greet the camp directors who stood on the dock with welcoming hands outstretched. Last of all came the new girls, looking about them inquiringly, and already beginning to fall in love with the place.

Hildegard G. Frey

CHAPTER II

GETTING SETTLED

Along the bluff overlooking the river, and half buried in the pine trees, stretched a long, low, rustic building, the pillars of whose wide piazza were made of tree trunks with the bark left on. A huge chimney built of cobblestones almost covered the one end. The great pines hovered over it protectingly; their branches caressing its roof as they waved gently to and fro in the light breeze. On the peak of one of its gables a little song sparrow, head tilted back and body a-tremble, trilled forth an ecstasy of song.

"Isn't it be-yoo-tiful?" sighed Hinpoha, her artistic soul delighting in the lovely scene before her. "I wonder what that house is for?"

"I don't know," replied Sahwah, equally enchanted. "There's another house behind it, farther up on the hill."

This second house was much larger than the bungalow overhanging the water's edge; it, too, was built in rustic fashion, with tree-trunks for porch posts; it was long and rambling, and had an additional story at the back, where the hill sloped away.

It was into this latter house that the crowd of girls was pouring, and the Winnebagos, following the others, found themselves in a large dining room, open on three sides to the veranda, and screened all around the open space. On the fourth side was an enormous fireplace built of stones like those they had seen in the chimney of the other house. Over its wide stone shelf were the words CAMP KEEWAYDIN traced in small, glistening blue pebbles in a cement panel. Although the day was hot, a small fire of paper and pine knots blazed on the hearth, crackling a cheery welcome to the newcomers as they entered. In the center of the room two long tables and a smaller one were set for dinner, and from the regions below came the appetizing odor of meat cooking, accompanied by the portentous clatter of an egg beater.

There was apparently an attic loft above the dining-room, for next to the chimney a square opening showed in the raftered ceiling, with a ladder leading up through it, fastened against the wall below. Up this ladder a dozen or more of the younger girls scrambled as soon as they entered the room; laughing, shrieking, tumbling over each other in their haste; and after a moment of thumping and bouncing about, down they all came dancing, clad in middies and bloomers, and raced, whooping like Indians, down the path which led to the tents.

"Are we supposed to get into our bloomers right away?" Oh-Pshaw whispered to Agony. "Ours are in the trunk, and it hasn't been brought up yet."

"I don't believe we are," Agony returned, watching Mary Sylvester, who stood talking to Pom-pom in the doorway of the Camp Director's office. "None of the older girls are doing it; just the youngsters."

Just then Mrs. Grayson, the Camp Director's wife, came out of the office and announced that dinner would be served immediately, after which the tent assignments would be made. The Winnebagos found themselves seated in a row down the side of one of the long tables, being served by a jolly-looking, muscular-armed councilor, who turned out to be the Camp Director's daughter, and who had her section of the table feeling at home in no time.

"Seven of you from one city!" she remarked to the Winnebagos, when she had called the roll of "native heaths," as she put it. "That's one of the largest delegations we have here. You all look like star campers, too," she added, sizing them up shrewdly. "Seven stars!" she repeated, evidently pleased with her simile. "We'll have to call you the Pleiades. We already have the Nine Muses from New York, the Twelve Apostles from Boston, the Heavenly Twins from Chicago and the Three Graces from Minneapolis, beside the Lone Wolf from Labrador, the Kangaroo from Australia, and the Elephant's Child from India."

"Oh, how delicious!" cried Sahwah delightedly. "Do you really mean that there are girls here from Australia and India?" Sahwah set down her water glass and gazed incredulously at Miss Judith. Miss Judith nodded over the pudding she was dishing up.

"The Kangaroo and the Lone Wolf are councilors," she replied, "but the Elephant's Child is a girl, the daughter of a missionary to India. She goes to boarding school here in America in the winter time, and always spends her summers at our camp. That is she, sitting at the end of the other table next to mother."

The Winnebagos glanced with quick interest to see what the girl from India might be like, and somewhat to their surprise saw that she was no different from the others. They recognized her as one of the younger girls who had been hanging over Pom-pom on the boat.

"Oh - she!" breathed Agony.

"What is her name?" asked Hinpoha, feeling immensely drawn to the girl, not because she came from India, but because she was even stouter than herself.

"Her name is Bengal Virden," replied Miss Judith.

"Bengal?" repeated Sahwah. "What an odd name. I suppose she was born in Bengal?"

"Yes, she was born there," replied Miss Judith. "She is a rather odd child," she continued, "but an all round good sport. Her mother died when she was small and she was brought up by her father until she was old enough to be sent to America, and since then she has divided her time between boarding schools and summer camps. She has a very affectionate nature, and gets tremendous crushes on the people she likes. Last summer it was Pom-pom, and she nearly wore her out with her adoration, although Pom-pom likes that sort of thing."

"Who is Pom-pom?" asked Agony curiously. "I have heard her name mentioned so many times."

"Pom-pom is our dancing teacher," replied Miss Judith. "She is the pretty councilor over there at the lower end of mother's table. All the girls get violent crushes on her," she continued, looking the Winnebagos over with a quizzical eye, as if to say that it would only be a short time before they, too, would be lying at Pom-pom's feet, another band of adoring slaves. Without knowing why, Agony suddenly felt unaccountably foolish under Miss Judith's keen glance, and taking her eyes from Pom-pom, she let them rove leisurely over the long line of girls at her own table.

"Who is the girl sitting third from the end on this side?" she asked, indicating the heavy-jawed individual who had made the impolite remark on the boat about Hinpoha, and who had just now pushed back her pudding dish with an emphatic movement after tasting one spoonful, and had turned to her neighbor with a remark which made the one addressed glance uncomfortably toward the councilor who was serving that section.

Miss Judith followed Agony's glance. "That," she replied in a non-committal tone, "is Jane Pratt. Will anyone have any more pudding?"

The pudding was delicious - chocolate with custard sauce - and Miss Judith was immediately busy refilling a half dozen dishes all proffered her at once. Agony made a mental note that Miss Judith had made no comment whatever upon Jane Pratt, although she had evidently been in camp the year before, and she drew her own conclusions about Jane's popularity.

"Who is Mary Sylvester?" Agony asked presently.

"Mary Sylvester," repeated Miss Judith in a tone which caught the attention of all the Winnebagos, it was so full of affection. "Mary Sylvester is the salt of the earth," Miss Judith continued warmly. "She's the brightest, loveliest, most kind-hearted girl I've ever met, and I've met a good many. She can't help being popular; she's as jolly as she is pretty, and as unassuming as she is talented. For an all around good camper 'we will never see her equal, though we search the whole world through,' as the camp song runs."

Agony looked over to where Mary Sylvester sat, the center of an animated group, and yearned with all her heart to be so prominent and so much noticed.

"I heard someone on the boat say that she would probably get the Buffalo Robe this year; that she had almost gotten it last year," continued Agony. "What is the Buffalo Robe, please?"

"The Buffalo Robe," replied Miss Judith, "is a large leather skin upon which the chief events of each camping season are painted in colors, and at the end of the summer it goes to the girl who is voted the most popular. She keeps it through the winter and returns it to us when camp opens the next year."

"Oh-h," breathed Agony, mightily interested. "And who got it last year?"

"Peggy Atterbury," said Miss Judith. "You'll hear all about her before very long. All the old girls are going to tie black ribbons on their tent poles tomorrow morning because she isn't coming back this year. She was another rare spirit like Mary Sylvester, only a bit more prominent, because she saved a girl from drowning one day."

Agony's heart swelled with ambition and desire as she listened to Miss Judith telling about the Buffalo Robe. A single consuming desire burned in her soul - to win that Buffalo Robe. Nothing else mattered now; no other laurel she might possibly win held out any attraction; she must carry off the great honor. She would show Nyoda what a great quality of leadership she possessed; there would be no question of Nyoda's making her a Torch Bearer when she came home with the Buffalo Robe. Thus her imagination soared until she pictured herself laying the significant trophy at Nyoda's feet and heard Nyoda's words of congratulation. A sudden doubt assailed her in the midst of her dream.

"Do new girls ever win the Buffalo Robe?" she asked in a voice which she tried hard to make sound disinterested.

"Yes, certainly," replied Miss Judith. "Peggy Atterbury was a new girl last year, and the girl who won it the year before last was a new girl also."

Her doubt thus removed, Agony returned to her pleasant day dream with greater longing than ever. The conversation at their table was interrupted by shouts from the next group.

"Oh, Miss Judy, please, please, can't we live in the Alley?"

Another group farther down the table took up the cry, and the room echoed with clamorous requests to live either "in the Alley" or "on the Avenue." The Elephant's Child came in at the end with a fervent plea: "Please, can't I be in Pom-pom's tent *this* year?"

"Tent lists are all made out," replied Miss Judith blandly. "You'll all find out in a few moments where you're to be." She sat calmly amid the buzz of excited speculation.

Hildegard G. Frey

"What do they mean by living 'in the Alley'?" asked Sahwah curiously.

"There are two rows of tents," replied Miss Judith. "The first one is called the Avenue and the second one the Alley. This end of camp, where the bungalows are, is known as the Heights, and the other end the Flats. There is always a great rivalry in camp between the dwellers in the Alley and the dwellers on the Avenue, and the two compete for the championship in sports."

"Oh, how jolly!" cried Sahwah eagerly. "Where are we to be?" she continued, filled with a sudden burning desire to live in the Alley.

"You'll know soon," said Miss Judith, with another one of her quizzical smiles, and with that the Winnebagos had to be content.

In a few moments dinner was finished and Mrs. Grayson rose and read the tent assignments. The tents all had names, it appeared; there was Bedlam and Avernus, Jabberwocky, Hornets, Nevermore, Gibraltar, Tamaracks, Fairview, Woodpeckers, Ravens, All Saints, Aloha, and a number of others which the Winnebagos could not remember at one hearing. Three girls and one councilor were assigned to each tent. Sahwah and Agony and Hinpoha heard themselves called to go to Gitchee-Gummee; Gladys and Migwan were put with Bengal Virden, the Elephant's Child from India, into a tent called Ponemah; while Katherine and Oh-Pshaw were assigned, without any tentmate, to "Bedlam." The Winnebagos smiled involuntarily when this last assignment was read, knowing how well Katherine's erratic nature befitted the name of the place. Gitchee-Gummee, Sahwah found to her delight, was the tent nearest the woods; next to it, but on the other side of a small gully, spanned by a rustic bridge, came Aloha, Pom-pom's tent; on the other side of Aloha stood Ponemah, in the shadow of twin pines of immense height; while Bedlam was farther along in the same row, just beyond

Avernus. Avernus, the Winnebagos noticed to their amusement, was a tent pitched in a deep hollow, the approach to which was a rocky passage down a steep hillside, strikingly suggestive of the classical entrance way to the nether regions. Only the ridgepole of Avernus was visible from the level upon which Bedlam stood, all the rest of it being hidden by the high rocks which surround it. Bedlam, on the other hand, was built on a height, and commanded a view of nearly all the other tents, being itself a conspicuous object in the landscape.

To their secret joy, the Winnebagos saw that their tents were all in the back row, in the Alley. Agony, especially, was exultant, since she saw that Mary Sylvester was also in the Alley. Mary was in Aloha, Pom-pom's tent, right next door, and Agony had a feeling that wherever Mary Sylvester was, there would be the center of things, and being right next door might have its advantages.

"We're going to have Miss Judith for a councilor," remarked Sahwah joyfully, as she dumped her armful of blankets down on one of the beds - the one on the side toward the woods.

"I wonder which bed she would like," said Hinpoha, standing irresolutely in the center of the floor with her armful of bedding.

"Here she comes now," announced Agony. "Let's wait and ask her."

"Well, she wouldn't want *this* one anyway," remarked Sahwah, as she straightened the mattress on her bed preparatory to spreading the sheets, "it sags in the middle like everything. I didn't take the best one if I did take first choice" - a fact which was apparent to all.

Bedlam's councilor, who had been announced as Miss Armstrong, from Australia, had already staked her claim when Katherine and Oh-Pshaw arrived, although she herself was nowhere in sight. One of the beds was made up and covered with a blanket of such dazzling gorgeousness that the two girls were almost blinded, and after one look turned their eyes outdoors for relief. All colors of the rainbow ran riot in that blanket, each one trying to outdo the others in brilliancy and intensity, until the effect was a veritable Vesuvius eruption of infernal splendors.

"Think of having to live with *that*!" exclaimed Oh-Pshaw tragically. "My eyesight will be ruined in one day. Imagine the effect after I get out my pink and gray one."

"And my lavender one!" added Katherine.

"We won't ever dare roll up the sides of our tent," continued Oh-Pshaw. "We'll look like a beacon fire, up here on this hill. Our tent is visible from the whole camp."

"Cheer up," said Katherine philosophically, "maybe there are others just as bad. Anyway, let's not act as if we minded; it might make Miss Armstrong feel badly. She probably thinks it's handsome, or she wouldn't have it. Coming from Australia that way, she may have quite savage tastes."

"I wonder what she'll be like," ruminated Oh-Pshaw, standing on one foot to tie the sneaker she had just substituted for her high traveling shoe.

As if in answer to her wondering, a clear, far-carrying call came to the ears of both girls at that moment. "Coo-*ee*! Coo-*ee*! Coo-*ee*"

"What is that?' asked Oh-Pshaw, pausing in her shoe lacing with one foot poised airily in space.

The call was repeated just outside their tent door, and then trailed off into silence.

"Is that someone calling to us?" asked Katherine, hurriedly pulling her middy on over her head and throwing back the tent flap. No one was in sight outside.

"Must have been for someone else," she reported, looking right and left along the pathway. "There's nobody out here."

She came back into the tent and began arranging her small possessions on the shelf which swung overhead.

"How I'm ever going to keep all my things on one-third of this shelf is more -" she began, but her speech ended in a startled gasp, for the floor of the tent suddenly heaved up in the center, sending bottles, brushes and boxes tumbling in all directions. The board which had thus heaved up so miraculously continued to rise at one end, and underneath it a pair of long, lean, powerful-looking arms came into view, followed by a head and a pair of shoulders. Katherine and Oh-Pshaw sat petrified at the apparition.

"Did I scare you, girls?" asked a deep, strong voice, and the apparition looked gravely from one to the other. It was a dark-skinned face, bronzed by wind and weather to a coppery, Indian-like tinge, and the hair which framed it was coarse and black. Only the head and shoulders of the apparition were visible beside the arms, the rest being concealed in the depths underneath the tent, but the breadth of those shoulders indicated clearly what might be expected in the way of a body. After a moment of roving back and forth between the two girls, the dark eyes under the heavy eyebrows fastened themselves upon Katherine with a mournful intensity of gaze that held her spellbound, speechless. After a full moment's scrutiny the dark eyes dropped, and the apparition, using her arms as levers, raised herself to the level of the floor and stood up. She was taller even than they had expected from the breadth of her shoulders; in fact, she seemed taller than the tent itself. Katherine, who up until that moment had considered herself tall, felt like a pigmy beside her, or, as she expressed it, "like Carver Hill suddenly set down beside one of the Alps." Never had she seen such a monumental young woman; such suggestion of strength and vigor contained in a feminine frame.

Oh-Pshaw looked timidly at the human Colossus standing in the middle of the tent, and inquired meekly, "Are you Miss Armstrong? Are you our Councilor?"

"I am," replied the newcomer gravely, replacing the board in the floor with a nonchalance which conveyed the impression that coming up through floors was her usual manner cf entering places.

"Why did you come in that way?" burst out Katherine, unable to contain her curiosity any longer.

"Oh, I just happened to be under the tent," replied Miss Armstrong, speaking in a drawling voice with a marked English accent, "looking for the broom, when I spied that loose board and thought I'd come in that way. It was less trouble than coming cut and going around to the steps."

"Less trouble," echoed Katherine. "I should think it would have been more trouble raising that heavy board with my suitcase standing on it."

"Was your suitcase on it?" inquired Miss Armstrong casually. "I didn't notice."

"Didn't notice!" repeated Katherine in astonishment. "It weighs thirty pounds."

"I weigh two hundred and thirty," returned Miss Armstrong conversationally.

"You do!" exclaimed Katherine in amazement. "You certainly don't look it." Indeed, it seemed incredible that Miss Armstrong, tall as she was, could possibly weigh so much, for she looked lean and gaunt as a wolf hound.

"You must be awfully strong, to have raised that board,"

Katherine continued, squinting at the muscular brown arms, which seemed solid as iron.

For answer Miss Armstrong took a step forward, picked Katherine up as if she had been a feather, threw her over her shoulder like a sack of potatoes, held her there for a moment head downward, and then swung her up and set her lightly on the hanging shelf, while Oh-Pshaw looked on round-eyed and open-mouthed with astonishment.

Just then a shadow appeared in the doorway, and Katherine looked down to see a shrinking little figure with pipestem legs standing on the top step.

"Hello!" Katherine called gaily, from her airy perch. "Are you our neighbor from Avernus? Do you want anything?" she added, for the girl was swallowing nervously, and seemed to be on the verge of making a request.

"Will somebody please show me how to make a bed?" faltered the visitor in a thin, piping voice. "It isn't made, and I don't know how to do it."

"Daggers and dirks!" exploded Katherine, nearly falling off the shelf under the stress of her emotion.

"What's the matter with the rest of the folks in Avernus - can't they make beds either?" asked Miss Armstrong, surveying the wisp of a girl in the doorway with an intent, solemn gaze that sent her into a tremble of embarrassment.

"My 'tenty' hasn't come yet," she faltered in reply.

"Who's your councilor?"

"I don't know; she isn't there." The voice broke on the last words, and the blue eyes overflowed with tears.

Katherine leaped from the shelf to the bed and down to the

floor. "I'll come over and help you make your bed," she said kindly.

"All right," said Miss Armstrong, nodding gravely. "You go over with her and I'll find out who's councilor in Avernus and send her around."

To herself she added, when the other two were out of earshot, "Baby's away from it's mother for the first time, and it's homesick."

"Poor thing," said Oh-Pshaw, who had overheard Miss Armstrong's remark.

"She'll get over it," replied Miss Armstrong prophetically.

If Miss Armstrong was a novelty to the tenants of Bedlam, the councilor in Poneman also seemed an odd character to the three girls she was to chaperon - only she was a much less agreeable surprise. She was a stout, fussy woman of about forty with thick eye-glasses which pinched the corners of her eyes into a strained expression. She greeted the girls briefly when they presented themselves to her, and in the next breath began giving orders about the arrangement of the tent. The beds must stand thus and so; the washstand must be on the other side from where it was; the mirror must stay on this side. And she must have half of the swinging shelf for her own; she could not possibly do with less; the others could get along as best they might with what was left.

"We're supposed to divide the shelf up equally," announced Bengal Virden, who had begun to look upon Miss Peckham - that was her name - with extreme disapproval from the moment of their introduction. Bengal was a girl whose every feeling was written plainly upon her face; she could not mask her emotions under an inscrutable countenance. Her dislike of Miss Peckham was so evident that Migwan and Gladys had expected an outbreak before this; but Bengal had merely stood scowling while the beds were being moved about. With the episode of the swinging shelf, however, she flared into open defiance.

"We're all to have an equal share of the shelf," she repeated.

"Nonsense," replied Miss Peckham in an emphatic tone. "I'm a councilor and I need more space."

Bengal promptly burst into tears. "I want to be in Pom-pom's tent!" she wailed, and fled from the scene, to throw herself upon Pom-pom in the next tent and pour out her tale of woe.

Migwan and Gladys looked at each other rather soberly as they went out to fill their water pitcher.

"What a strange person to have as councilor," ventured Gladys. "I thought councilors at camps were always as sweet as they could be. Miss Peckham looks as though she could be horrid without half trying."

"Maybe it's just her way, though," replied Migwan good temperedly. "She may be very nice inside after we get to know her. She's probably never been a councilor before, and thinks she must show her authority."

"Authority!" cried Gladys. "But we're not babies; we're grown up. I'm afraid she's not going to be a very agreeable proctor."

"Oh, well," replied Migwan gently, "let's make the best of her and have a good time anyway. We mustn't let her spoil our fun for us. We'll probably find something to like in her before long."

"I wish I had your angelic disposition," sighed Gladys, "but I just can't like people when they rub me the wrong way, and Miss Peckham does that to me."

"There's going to be trouble with the Elephant's Child," remarked Migwan soberly. "She has already taken a strong dislike to Miss Peckham, and she is still childish enough to show it."

"Yes, I'm afraid there will be trouble between Bengal and Miss Peckham," echoed Gladys, "and we'll be constantly called upon to make peace. It's a role I'm not anxious for."

"Let's not worry about it beforehand," said Migwan, charmed into a blissful attitude of mind toward the whole world by the sheer beauty of the scene that unrolled before her. The river, tinged by the long rays of the late afternoon sun, gleamed like a river of living gold, blinding her eyes and setting her to dreaming of magic seas and far countries. She stood very still for many minutes, lost in golden fancies, until Gladys took her gently by the arm.

"Come, Migwan, are you going to day-dream here forever? There is the spring we are looking for, just at the end of that little path."

Migwan came slowly out of her reverie and followed Gladys down the hill to the spring.

"It's all so beautiful," she sighed in ecstasy, turning to look back once more at the shimmering water, "it just makes me *ache*. It makes everything unworthy in me want to crawl away and lose itself, while everything good in me wants to sing. Don't you feel that way about it, too?"

"Something like that," replied Gladys softly. "When Nature is so lovely, it makes me want to be lovely, too, to match. I don't see how anyone could ever be angry here, or selfish, or mean. It's just like being made over, with all the bad left out."

"It does seem that way,' replied Migwan.

"Here is the spring!" cried both girls in unison, as they reached the end of the path and came upon a deep, rocky basin, filled with crystal clear water that gushed out from the rock above their heads, trickling down through ferns to be caught and held in the pool below, so still and shining that it reflected the faces of the two girls like a mirror.

"Oh-h!" breathed Migwan in rapture, sinking down among the ferns and lilies that bordered the spring and dabbling her fingers in the limpid water, "I feel just like a wood-nymph, or a naiad, or whatever those folks were that lived by the springs and fountains in the Greek mythology."

Withdrawing her fingers from the water and clasping her hands loosely around her knees, she began to recite idly:

> "Dian white-armed has given me this cool shrine,
> Deep in the bosom of a wood of pine;
> The silver sparkling showers
> That hive me in, the flowers
> That prink my fountain's brim, are hers and mine;
> And when the days are mild and fair,
> And grass is springing, buds are blowing,
> Sweet it is, 'mid waters flowing,
> Here to sit and know no care,
> 'Mid the waters flowing, flowing, flowing,
> Combing my yellow, yellow hair."

"That poem must have been written about this very place," she added, dreamily gazing into the shadowy depths of the pool beside her.

"Who wrote it?" inquired Gladys.

"I've forgotten," replied Migwan. "I learned it once in Literature, a long time ago."

Both girls were silent, gazing meditatively into the pool, like *gazing* into a future-revealing crystal, each absorbed in her own day dreams. They were startled by the sound of a clear, musical piping, coming apparently from the tangle of bushes behind them. Now faint, now louder, it swelled and died away on the breeze, now fairly startling in its joyousness, now plaintive as the wind sighing among the reeds in some lonely spot after nightfall; alluring, thrilling, mocking by turns; elusive as the strains of fairy pipers; utterly ravishing in its sweetness.

Migwan and Gladys lifted their heads and looked at each other in wonder.

"Pipes of Pan!" exclaimed Migwan, and both girls glanced around, half expecting to see the graceful form of a faun gliding toward them among the trees. Nothing was to be seen, but the piping went on, merrily as before, rising, falling, swelling, dying away in the distance, breaking out again at near hand.

"Oh, what *is* it?" cried Gladys. "Is it a bird?"

"It can't be a bird," replied Migwan, "it's a *tune - sort* of a tune. No, I wouldn't exactly call it a tune, either, but it's different from a bird call. It sounds like pipes - fairy pipes - Pipes of Pan. Oh-h-h! Just *listen*! What *can* it be?"

The clear tones had leaped a full octave, and with a mingled sound of pipes and flutes went trilling deliriously on a high note until the listeners held their breath with delight. Then abruptly the piping stopped, ending in a queer, unfinished way that tantalized their ears for many minutes afterward, and held them motionless, spellbound, waiting for the strain to be resumed. They listened in vain; the mysterious piper called no more. Soon afterward a bugle pealed forth, sounding the mess call, and coming to earth with a start, the two girls raced back to Ponemah with their water pitcher and then hastened on into the dining room, where the campers, now all clad in regulation blue bloomers and white middies, were already assembled.

CHAPTER III

THE GREAT MYSTERY SOUND

After supper the camp was summoned to the smaller bungalow for first assembly and Sing-Out. Over the wide entrance doorway of this picturesque building among the trees was painted in large ornamental letters:

MATEKA

THE HOUSE OF JOYOUS LEARNING

This house, Dr. Grayson explained, was the place where all the craft work was to be done. The light from the lamps fell upon beautifully decorated board walls; wood-blocked curtains, quaint rustic benches and seats made from logs with the bark left on; flower-holders fashioned of birch bark; candlesticks of hammered brass, silver and copper; book covers of beaded leather; vases and bowls of glazed clay.

At one end of the long room stood a piano; at the other end was the huge cobblestone fireplace whose chimney the Winnebagos had noticed from the outside; in it a fire was laid ready for lighting.

The seventy-five girls filed in and seated themselves on the floor, looking expectantly at Dr. Grayson, who stood before the fireplace. He was an imposing figure as he stood there, a man over six feet tall, with a great head of white hair like a lion's mane, which, emphasizing the ruddy complexion and clear blue eyes, contrived to make him look youthful instead of old.

In a beautiful speech, full of both wisdom and humor, he explained the ideals of camp life, and heartily welcomed the group before him into the family circle of Camp Keewaydin. He spoke of the girls who in past years had stood out from the others on account of their superior camp spirit, and led up to the subject of the Buffalo Robe, which at the end of the season would be awarded to the one who should be voted by her fellow campers as the most popular girl.

A solemn hush fell over the assembly as he spoke, and all eyes were fastened upon the Buffalo Robe, hanging over the fireplace. Agony's heart gave a leap at the sight of the beautiful trophy, and then sank as she saw innumerable eyes turn to rest upon Mary Sylvester, sitting on a low stool at Dr. Grayson's feet, gazing up at him with a look of worship in her expressive eyes.

When he had finished speaking of the Buffalo Robe Dr. Grayson announced that the first fire of the season was to be lighted in the House of Joyous Learning to dedicate it to this year's group of campers, and kneeling down on the hearth, he touched off the faggots laid ready in the fireplace, and the flames, leaping and snapping, rose up the chimney, sending a brilliant glow over the room, and causing the most homesick youngster to brighten up and feel immensely cheered.

The fire lighted, and the House of Joyous Learning dedicated to its present occupants, Dr. Grayson proceeded to introduce the camp leaders and councilors. Mrs. Grayson came first, as Camp Mother and Chief Councilor. She was a large woman, and seemed capable of mothering the whole world as she sat before the hearth, beaming down upon the girls clustered around her on the floor, and there was already a note of genuine affection in the voices of the new girls as they joined in the cheer which the old girls started in honor of the

Camp Mother.

The cheer was not yet finished when there was a sound of footsteps on the porch outside and a new girl stood in the doorway. She carried a blanket over one arm and held a small traveling bag in her hand. Her face was flushed with exertion and her chest heaved as she stood there looking inquiringly about the room with merry eyes that seemed to be delighted with everything they looked upon. Her face was round; her little button mouth was round; the comical stub of a nose which perched above it gave the effect of being round, too, while the deep dimple that indented her chin was very, *very* round. Two still deeper dimples lurked in her cheeks, each one a silent chuckle, and the freckles that clustered thickly over her features all seemed to twinkle with a separate and individual hilarity.

An involuntary smile spread over the faces inside the bungalow as they looked at the newcomer, and one of the younger girls laughed aloud. That was the signal for a general laugh, and for a moment the room rang, and the strange girl in the doorway joined in heartily, and Dr. Grayson laughed, too, and everybody felt "wound up" and hilarious. Mrs. Grayson left her chair by the hearth and made her way through the group of girls on the floor to the newcomer, holding out her hand in welcome.

"You must be Jean Lawrence," she said, drawing the girl into the room. "You were to arrive by automobile at Green's Landing this noon, were you not, and come across the river in the mail boat? I have been wondering why you did not arrive on that boat."

"Our automobile broke down on that road that runs through the long woods beyond Green's Landing," replied Jean, "and when father found it could not be fixed on the road he decided to go back to the last town we had passed through and spend the night there; so I had to walk to Green's Landing. It was nearly nine miles and it took me all afternoon to get there. The mail boat had, of course, gone long ago, but a nice old grandpa man brought me over in a row boat."

"You walked nine miles to Green's Landing!" exclaimed Mrs. Grayson in astonishment. "But, my dear, why didn't you wait and let your father drive you down in the morning?"

"Oh, I wouldn't miss a single night in camp for anything in the world!" replied Jean. "I would have walked if it had been *twenty*-nine miles. I nearly died of impatience before I got here, as it was!"

Mrs. Grayson beamed on the enthusiastic camper; the old girls sang a lusty cheer to the new girl who was such a good sport; and, twinkling and beaming in all directions, Jean sat down on the floor with the others to hear the camp councilors introduced.

Dr. Grayson began by quoting humorously from the Proverbs: "Where no council is, the people fall, but in a multitude of councilors there is safety."

One by one he called the councilors up and introduced them, beginning with his daughter Judith, who was to be gymnastic director at the camp. Miss Judy got up and made a bow, and then prepared to sit down again, but her father would not let her off so easily. He demanded a demonstration of her profession for the benefit of the campers. Miss Judy promptly lined all the other councilors up and put them through a series of ridiculous exercises, such as "Tongues forward thrust!" "Hand on pocket place!" "Handkerchief take!" "Noses blow!" - performance which was greeted with riotous applause by the campers.

Miss Armstrong was called up next and introduced as "our little friend from Australia, the swimming teacher, who, on account of her diminutive size goes by the nickname of Tiny." Tiny was made to give her native Australian bush call of "Coo-ee! Coo-ee!" and was then told to rescue a drowning person in pantomime, which she did so realistically that the campers sat in shivering fascination. Tiny, still grave and unsmiling, sat down amid shouts for encore, and refused to repeat her performance, pretending to be overcome with bashfulness. Dr. Grayson then rose and said that since Tiny was too modest to appear in public herself, he would bring out her most cherished possession to respond to the encore, and held up the gaudy blanket that Katherine and Oh-Pshaw had already made merry over in the tent, explaining that Tiny always chose quiet, dull colors to match her retiring nature. With a teasing twinkle in his eyes he handed Tiny her blanket and then passed on to the next victim.

This was Pom-pom, the dancing teacher, who was obliged to do a dance on the piano stool to illustrate her art. Pom-pom received a perfect ovation, especially from the younger girls, and was called out half a dozen times.

"Oh, the sweet thing! The darling!" gushed Bengal Virden, going into a perfect ecstasy on the floor beside Gladys. "Don't you just *adore* her?"

"She's very pretty," replied Gladys sincerely.

"Pretty!" returned Bengal scornfully. "She's the most beautiful person on earth! Oh, I love her so, I don't know what to *do*!"

Gladys smiled indulgently at Bengal's gush, and turned away to see Jane Pratt's dull, unpleasant eyes gazing contemptuously upon Pom-pom's performance, and heard her whisper to her neighbor, "She's too stiff-legged to be really graceful."

The Lone Wolf from Labrador, summoned to stand up and show herself next, was a long, lean, mournful-looking young woman who, when introduced, explained in a lugubrious voice that she had no talents like the rest of the councilors and didn't know enough to be a teacher of anything; but she was very good and pious, and had been brought to camp solely for her moral effect upon the other councilors.

For a moment the camp girls looked at the Lone Wolf in silence, not knowing what to make of her; then Sahwan noticed that Mrs. Grayson was biting her lips, while her eyes twinkled; Dr. Grayson was looking at the girls with a quizzical expression on his face; Miss Judy had her face buried in her handkerchief. Sahwah looked back at the Lone Wolf, standing there with her hands folded angelically and her eyes fixed solemnly upon the ceiling, and she suddenly snorted out with laughter. Then everyone caught on and laughed, too, but the Lone Wolf never smiled; she stood looking at them with an infinitely sad, pained expression that almost convinced them that she had been in earnest.

The Lone Wolf, it appeared, was to be Tent Inspector, and when that announcement was made, the laughter of the old girls turned to groans of pretended aversion, which increased to a mighty chorus when Dr. Grayson added that her eye had never been known to miss a single detail of disorder in a tent.

Thus councilor after councilor was introduced in a humorous speech by Dr. Grayson, and made to do her particular stunt, or was rallied about her pet hobby. The two Arts and Crafts teachers were given lumps of clay and a can of house paint and ordered to produce a statue and a landscape respectively; the Sing Leader had to play "Darling, I Am Growing Old" on a pitch pipe, and all the plain "tent councilors" were called upon for a "few remarks."

All were cheered lustily, and all gave strong evidence of future popularity except Miss Peckham, who drew only a very scattered and perfunctory applause. Gladys and Migwan, who glanced at each other as Miss Peckham stepped forward, were surprised to hear that she was Dr. Grayson's cousin.

"That accounts for her being here," Gladys whispered, and Migwan whispered in return, "We'll just have to make the best of her."

Bengal glowered at Miss Peckham and made no pretense of

applauding her, and Migwan saw her whispering to the group around her, and saw Bengal's expression of dislike swiftly reflected on the faces of her listeners. Thus, before Miss Peckham was fairly introduced, her unpopularity was already sealed. It takes very little to make a reputation at camp. Estimates are formed very swiftly, and great attachments and antipathies are formed at first sight. Young girls seem to scent, by some mysterious intuition, who is really in sympathy with them, and who is only pretending to be, and bestow or withhold their affections accordingly. In the code of the camp girl classifications are very simple; a camper is either a "peach" or a "prune." All the other councilors were "peaches"; that was the instantaneous verdict of the Keewaydin Campers during the introductions; Miss Peckham, regardless of the fact that she was Dr. Grayson's cousin, was a "prune."

The last councilor to be introduced was a handsome, white-haired woman named Miss Amesbury, who was introduced as the patron saint of the camp, the designer of the beautiful Mateka, the House of Joyous Learning. Miss Amesbury was neither an instructor nor a tent councilor; she had just come to be a friend and helper to the whole camp, and lived on the second story balcony of Mateka. Word had traveled around among the girls that she was a famous author, and a ripple of expectation agitated the ranks of the campers as she rose in answer to Dr. Grayson's summons. Migwan gazed upon her in mingled awe and veneration. A famous author - one who had realized the ambition that was also her cherished own! She almost stopped breathing in her emotion.

"Isn't she lovely?" breathed Hinpoha to Agony, her eye taking in the details of Miss Amesbury's camping suit, which, instead of being made of serge or khaki, like those of the other councilors, was of heavy Japanese silk, with a soft, flowered tie.

Smiling a smile which included every girl in the room, she cordially invited them all to come and visit her balcony and share the beautiful view which she had of the river and the gorge. Then she added a few humorous comments upon camp life, and sat down amid tumultuous applause.

Then Dr. Grayson asked her if she would play for the singing, and she rose graciously and took her place at the piano. The Sing leader stood up on a bench and directed with a wooden spoon from the craft table, and the first Sing-Out began. For half an hour the mingled voices were lifted in glee and round, in part song and ballad, until the roof rang. The new girls, spelling out the words in the song books by the rather pale lamplight, came out strongly in some parts and wobbly in others, producing some tone effects which caused the old girls to double up with merriment, but the new girls showed their good sportsmanship by singing on lustily no matter how many mistakes they made, a fact which caused Dr. Grayson to beam approvingly upon them. In the midst of a particularly hilarious song the bugle suddenly blew for going to bed, and the old girls, still singing, began to drift out of the house and make for the tents in groups of twos and threes, with their arms thrown around each other's shoulders. The new girls followed, some feeling shy and a bit homesick this first night away from home; others already perfectly at home, their arms around a new friend made in the short time since their arrival. One such was Jean Lawrence, who, upon being informed that she was to be "tenty" to Katherine and Oh-Pshaw in Bedlam, expressed herself as being unutterably delighted with her tent mates and walked off with them chattering as easily as though she had known them all her life.

There was more or less confusion this first night before everyone got settled, for many of the girls had never camped before and were unskilled in the art of undressing rapidly in the close quarters of a tent, and "Taps" sounded before a number were even undressed. The Lone Wolf was lenient this first night, however, and did not insist upon prompt lights out, an act of grace which added greatly to her popularity.

Sahwah's bed sagged somewhat in the middle and she was not able to adjust herself to its curves very well; consequently she did not fall asleep soon. Camp quieted down; the last rustle and whisper died away; silence enfolded the tents around. Sahwah, lying wide awake in the darkness, her senses alert, heard the sound of footsteps running at full speed along the top of the bluff and across the bare rocks at the edge. Here the footsteps seemed to come to a pause, and an instant later there came a sound like a loud splash in the water below. Filled both with curiosity and apprehension, Sahwah leaped from bed and raced for the edge of the bluff, where she stood peering down at the river. No unusual ripple appeared on the placid surface of the river; as far as she could see it lay calm and peaceful in the moonlight.

A footstep behind her startled her, and she turned to see Miss Judy coming toward her from the tent.

"What's the matter?" called Miss Judy, when she was within a few yards of Sahwah.

"It sounded as though someone jumped off the cliff," replied Sahwah. "I heard footsteps along the edge of the bluff, and then a splash, and I ran out to see what was going on, but I can't see anything."

To Sahwah's surprise, Miss Judith laughed aloud. "Oh," she said, "did you hear it?"

"What was it?" asked Sahwah, curiously.

"That," replied Miss Judy, "is what we call the Great Mystery Sound. We hear it off and on, but no one has ever been able to explain what causes it. Our 'diving ghost,' we call it. Father wore himself to a frazzle the first year we were here, trying to find out what it was. He used to sit up nights and watch, but although he often heard it he never could see anything that could produce the sound. Some people about here have told us that that sound has been heard for years and they say that there is an old legend connected with it to the effect that many years ago an Indian girl, pursued by an unwelcome suitor, jumped off this bluff and drowned herself to escape him, and that ever

Hildegard G. Frey

since that occurrence this strange sound has been noticeable. Of course, the people who tell the legend say that the ghost of the persecuted maiden haunts the scene of the tragedy at intervals and repeats the performance. Whatever it is, we have never been able to account for the sound naturally, and always refer to it as the Great Mystery Sound."

"What a strange thing!" exclaimed Sahwah in wonder. "Those footsteps certainly sounded real; and as for that splash! It actually made my flesh creep. I had a panicky feeling that one of the new girls had wandered too near the edge of the bluff and had fallen into the water."

"It used to have that effect upon us at first, too," replied Miss Judy. "We would all come racing down here with our hearts in our mouths, expecting we knew not what. It took a long time before we could believe it was a delusion.

"And now, come back to bed, or you'll be taking cold, standing out here in your nightgown."

Still looking back at the river and half expecting to see some agitation in its surface, Sahwah followed Miss Judy back to Gitchee-Gummee and returned to bed.

CHAPTER IV

THE ALLEY INITIATION

Folk-dancing hour had just drawn to a close, and the long bugle for swimming sounded through camp. The sets of eight which had been drawn up on the tennis court in the formation of "If All the World Were Paper," broke and scattered as before a whirlwind as the girls raced for their tents to get into bathing suits. Sahwah, as might be expected, was first down on the dock, but close at her heels was another girl whom she recognized as living in one of the Avenue tents. This girl, while broader and heavier than Sahwah, moved with the same easy grace that characterized Sahwah's movements, and like Sahwah, she seemed consumed with impatience to get into the water.

"Oh, I wish Miss Armstrong would hurry, hurry, hurry!" she exclaimed, jigging up and down on the dock. "I just can't wait until I get in."

"Neither can I," replied Sahwah, scanning the path down the hillside for a sight of the swimming director.

"Do you live in the Avenue or the Alley?" asked the girl beside her.

"In the Alley," replied Sahwah.

"Which tent?"

"Gitchee-Gummee. Which one are you in?"

"Jabberwocky."

"That's way up near the bungalow, isn't it?"

"Yes, where are you?"

"The very last tent in the Alley, that one there, buried in the trees."

"Oh, how lovely! You're right near the path to the river, aren't you? I wish I were a little nearer this end. It would save time getting to the water."

"But you're so near the bungalow that you only have to go a step when the breakfast bugle blows. You have the advantage there," replied Sahwah. "We down in Gitchee-Gummee have to run for all we're worth to get there before you're all assembled. We have hard work getting dressed in time. We put on our ties while we're running down the path, as it is."

The other girl laughed, showing a row of very white, even teeth. "Did you see that girl who came running into the dining-room this morning with her middy halfway over her head?"

Sahwah laughed, too, at the recollection. "That was Bengal Virden, the one they call the Elephant's Child," she replied. "She lives in Ponemah, with some friends of mine. She had loitered with her dressing and didn't have her middy on when the breakfast bugle blew, so she decided to put it on en route. But while she was pulling it on over her head she got stuck fast in it with her arms straight up in the air and had to come in that way and get somebody to pull her through. I never saw anything so funny," she finished.

"Neither did I," replied the other.

They looked at each other and laughed heartily at the remembrance of the ludicrous episode.

All this while Sahwah was trying to recollect her companion's name, but was unable to do so. It was impossible to remember which girls had answered to which names at the general roll call on that first night in Mateka.

Just then the other said, "I don't believe I recall your name - I'm very stupid about remembering things."

"That's just what I was going to say to you!" exclaimed Sahwah, with a merry laugh. "It's impossible to remember so many new names at once. I think we all ought to be labeled for the first week or so. I'm Sarah Ann Brewster, only they call me Sahwah."

"What a queer nickname! It's very interesting. Is it a contraction of Sarah Ann?"

"No, it's my Camp Fire name."

"Oh, are you a Camp Fire girl?"

"Yes."

"How splendid! I've always wished I could be one. What does the name mean?"

"Sunfish!" replied Sahwah. "The sun part means that I like sunshine and the fish part means that I like the water."

"Oh-h!" replied the other with an interested face. Then she began to introduce herself. "I haven't any nice symbolic name like yours," she said, "but mine is sort of queer, too."

"What is it?" asked Sahwah.

"Undine."

"Undine!" repeated Sahwah. "How lovely! I've always been perfectly crazy about Undine since I got the book on my tenth birthday. Undine was fond of water, like I was. What's the rest of your name?"

"Girelle," replied Undine.

"Do you live in the east or in the west?" asked Sahwah. "You don't speak like the Easterners, and yet you don't speak like us Westerners, either. What part of the country are you from?"

"No part at all," answered Undine. "My home is in Honolulu."

"Not really?" said Sahwah in astonishment.

"Really," replied Undine, smiling at Sahwah's look of surprise. "I was born in Hawaii, and I have lived there most of my life."

"Oh," said Sahwah, "I thought only Hawaiians lived in Hawaii - I didn't know anyone else was ever *born* there."

"Lots of white people are born there," replied Undine, politely checking the smile that wreathed her lips at Sahwah's ingenuous remark. "But," she added, "most of the people in the States seem to think no one lives in Hawaii but natives, and that they wear wreaths of flowers around their necks all the time and do nothing but play on ukuleles."

Sahwah laughed and made up her mind that she was going to like Undine very much. "I suppose you swim?" she asked, presently.

Undine nodded emphatically. "It's the thing I like to do best of anything in the world. Do you like it? Oh, yes, of course you do. You call yourself the Sunfish on that account."

Sahwah affirmed her love for the deep, and thrilled a little at discovering an enthusiasm to match hers in this girl from

Honolulu. The rest of the Winnebagos, although good swimmers, did not possess in an equal degree Sahwah's inborn passion for the water. Sahwah and Undine both felt the call of the river as it flowed past the dock; to each of them it beckoned with an irresistible invitation, until they could hardly restrain themselves from leaping off the boards into the cool, glassy depths below.

"Here comes Miss Armstrong!" shouted somebody at the other end of the dock, as the big Australian came into view down the path, and there was a scramble for the diving tower.

The swimming place at Camp Keewaydin was divided into three parts. A shallow cove at the left of the dock, where the curve of the river formed a tiny bay, was the sporting ground of the Minnows, the girls who could not swim at all; the Perch, or those who could swim a little, but were not yet sure of themselves, were assigned to the other side of the dock, where the water was slightly deeper, but where they were protected by the dock from the full force of the current; while the Sharks, the expert swimmers, were given the freedom of the river beyond the end of the pier. The diving tower was on the end of the pier and belonged exclusively to the Sharks; it was fifteen feet high, and had seven different diving boards placed at various heights. Besides the diving tower, there was a floating dock anchored out in midstream, having a springboard at either end. There was also a low diving board at the side of the pier for the Perch to practice on.

Miss Armstrong came down on the dock in a bright red bathing suit which shone brilliantly among the darker suits of the girls. She rapidly separated the Minnows from the other fish, and set them to learning their first strokes under the direction of one of the other councilors. Then she lined the remaining girls up for the test which would determine who were Sharks and who were Perch. The test consisted of a dive from any one of the diving boards of the tower and a demonstration of four standard strokes, ending up with a swim across the river and back.

About a dozen dropped out at the mere reading of the test and accepted their rating as Perch without a trial; as many more failed either to execute their dives properly or to give satisfaction in their swimming strokes. Sahwah, burning with impatience to show her skill, climbed nimbly up to the very top of the tower and went off the highest springboard in a neat back dive that drew applause from the watchers, including Miss Armstrong. She also passed the rest of the test with a perfect rating.

"You're the biggest Shark so far," remarked Miss Armstrong, as Sahwah clambered up on the dock after her swim across the river, during which she had almost outdistanced the boat which accompanied her over and back.

Sahwah smiled modestly as one of the old campers started a cheer for her, and turned to watch Undine Girelle, who was mounting the diving tower. When Undine also went off the highest springboard backward, and in addition turned a complete somersault before she touched the water, Sahwah realized that she had met her match, if not her master. Heretofore, Sahwah's swimming prowess had been unrivalled in whatever group she found herself, and it was a matter of course with the Winnebagos that Sahwah should carry off all honors in aquatics. Now they had to admit that in Undine Girelle Sahwah had a formidable rival and would have to look sharply to her laurels.

"Isn't she wonderful?" came in exclamations from all around, as Undine sported in the water like a dolphin. "But then," someone added, "she's used to bathing in the surf in Hawaii. No wonder."

There were about fifteen put in the Shark class in the first try-out, of whom Sahwah and Undine were acknowledged to be the best. Hinpoha and Gladys and Migwan also qualified as Sharks; Katherine went voluntarily into the Perch class, and Agony failed to pass her diving test, although she accomplished her distance swim and the demonstration of the strokes.

Agony felt somewhat humiliated at having to go into the second class; she would much rather have been in the more conspicuous Shark group. Sahwah had already made a reputation for herself; Hinpoha drew admiring attention when she let her glorious red curls down her back to dry them in the sun; but she herself had so far made no special impression upon the camp. Why hadn't she distinguished herself like Sahwah, or Undine Girelle, Agony thought enviously. Others were already fast on their way to becoming prominent, but so far she was still going unnoticed. Her spirit chafed within her at her obscurity.

Oh-Pshaw, alas, was only a Minnow. The fear of water which had lurked in her ever since the accident in her early childhood had kept her from any attempt to learn to swim. It was only since she had become a Winnebago and had once conquered her fear on that memorable night beside the Devil's Punch Bowl that she began to entertain the idea that some day she, too, might be at home in the water like the others. It was still a decided ordeal for her to go in; to feel the water flowing over her feet and to hear it splash against the piles of the dock and gurgle over the stones along the shore; but she resolutely steeled her nerves against the sound and the feel of the water, forcing back the terror that gripped her like an icy hand, and courageously tried to follow the director's instructions to put her face down under the surface. It was no use; she could not quite bring herself to do it; the moment the water struck her chin wild panic seized her and she would straighten up with a choking cry. She looked with envy at the other novices around her who fearlessly threw themselves into the water face downward, learning "Dead Man's Float" inside of ten minutes. She would never be able to do *that*, she reflected sorrowfully, as she climbed up on the dock before the period was half over, utterly worn out and discouraged by her repeated failures to bring her head under water.

Beside her on the dock sat a thin wisp of a girl whose bathing suit was not even wet.

"Didn't you go in?" asked Oh-Pshaw.

"No," replied the girl in a high, piping voice, and Oh-Pshaw recognized her as the dweller in Avernus who had come over that first day and asked them how to make her bed. Carmen Chadwick, they had found out her name was.

"I'm afraid of the water," continued Carmen. "Mamma never let me go in at home. She doesn't think it's quite ladylike for girls to swim."

Oh-Pshaw smiled in spite of herself. "Oh, I don't think it makes girls unladylike to learn how to swim," she defended. "It's considered to be a fine exercise; about the best there is to develop all the muscles."

"Oh!" said Carmen primly. "That's what mamma doesn't like, to have my muscles all lumpy and developed. She wants to keep me soft and curved."

Oh-Pshaw stifled a shriek with difficulty, and turning aside to hide her twinkling eyes she caught sight of the Lone Wolf standing on the dock not far away, gazing mournfully into the Minnow pond.

"What do you think of *her*?" asked Oh-Pshaw hastily, steering the conversation away from muscles and kindred unladylike topics.

"She's my Councy," replied Carmen.

"Your what?"

"My Councy - my Councilor. I'm frightened to death of her."

"Why, what does she do?" asked Oh-Pshaw in consternation.

"She doesn't do anything, in particular," replied Carmen. "She just stares at me solemn as an owl and every little while she puts her head down on her bed under the pillow. Do you know," she continued, sinking her voice to a whisper, "I believe there is something the matter with her mind."

"Really!" said Oh-Pshaw, her voice shaking ever so slightly.

"She doesn't seem to realize what she is saying, at all," said Carmen. "Do you remember when Dr. Grayson introduced her he said she was real good and pious, but she isn't a bit pious. She didn't bring any Bible with her and she didn't say any prayers before she went to bed."

"Maybe she said them to herself after she was in bed," remarked Oh-Pshaw, when she could control her voice again. "Lots of people do, you know."

"I don't believe she did," replied Carmen in a tone of conviction. "I watched her. She made shadow animals with her fingers on the tent wall in the moonlight the minute she got into bed, and she kept it up until she went to sleep."

Out of the corner of her eye Oh-Pshaw saw the Lone Wolf moving toward them, and hastily changed the subject. "Why did you put your bathing suit on when you didn't have any intention of going into the water?" she asked, seizing upon the first thing that came into her mind.

"It looks so well on me," replied Carmen. "Don't you think it does?"

"Y-yes, it d-does," admitted Oh-Pshaw, her teeth suddenly beginning to chatter, and she realized that she was sitting out too long in her wet bathing suit. "I g-guess I'll g-go up and get dressed," she finished, between the shivers that shook her like a reed.

The Lone Wolf came up to her and taking her own sweater off wrapped it around her and hustled her off toward her tent.

Hildegard G. Frey

Just then the cry of "All out!" sounded on the dock and the swimmers came flocking out of the water with many an exclamation of regret that the time was up.

"Oh, please, Tiny, may I do this one dive?" coaxed Bengal from one of the boards on the tower. "I'm all in a position to do it - see?"

"Time's up," replied Tiny inexorably, and Bengal reluctantly relinquished her dive and climbed down from the tower.

"Next test for Sharks a week from today!" called Tiny in her megaphone voice to the Perches, as she mounted the diving tower in preparation for her own initial plunge. The swimming instructors had their own swimming time after the girls were out of the water.

Gladys and Migwan were dripping their way back to Ponemah, one on either side of Bengal Virden, who was entertaining them with tales of former years at camp, when they were startled to see Miss Peckham standing on top of a high rock wildly waving them back.

"Don't go near the tent!" she shrieked.

"Why not?" called Migwan in alarm, as the three girls stood still in the path, the water which was dripping out of their bathing suits collecting in a puddle around their feet.

"There's a snake underneath the tent, a great big snake," answered Miss Peckham in terrified tones.

"Well, what of it?" demanded Bengal coolly. "I've seen lots of snakes. I'm not afraid of them. Come on, let's get a forked stick, and let's kill it."

She stooped to wring out the water which had collected in the bottom of her bathing suit and then started forward toward Ponemah.

Miss Peckham, high on her rock, raised a great outcry. "Stay where you are!" she commanded. "Don't you go near that tent."

Bengal kept on going, looking about her for a forked stick.

"Bengal *Virden!*" screamed Miss Peckham, in such a tone of terror that Bengal involuntarily stood still in her tracks, dropping the stick she was in the act of picking up. "It's a deadly poisonous snake," gasped Miss Peckham, beginning to get breathless from fright, "a monstrous black one with red rings on it. I saw it crawling among the leaves. It reared up and menaced me with its wicked head. Don't you stir another step!" she commanded as Bengal seemed on the point of going on.

"What's the matter?" asked a voice behind them, and there was Miss Judy, just coming out of her tent with her wet bathing suit in her hand.

"There's a terrible poisonous snake under our tent," replied Miss Peckham. "I was just coming out of the door after my nap when I saw it gliding underneath. It's down there now, under the bushes."

"How queer!" replied Miss Judy, looking with concern at her wildly excited cousin. "We've never had large snakes around here. What color did you say it was?"

"It had broad, alternate rings of red and black," replied Miss Peckham, with the air of one quoting from an authority, "the distinguishing marks of the coral snake, one of the seventeen poisonous reptiles out of the one hundred and eleven species of snakes found in the United States."

"A coral snake!" gasped Miss Judy, in real alarm, while the other three, taking fright from the tone of her voice, began to back down the path.

Other dwellers in the Alley came along to see what the commotion was about and were warned back in an important tone by Miss Peckham. The timid ones took to their heels and fled to the other end of camp, while the more courageous hung about as near as they dared come and stared fascinated at the miniature jungle of ferns and bushes that grew under Ponemah to a height of two or three feet. Sahwah, whose insatiable curiosity as usual got the better of her fears, climbed a tree quite close to Ponemah and peered down through the branches, all agog with desire to see the dread serpent show itself.

"Come down from there - quick!" called someone in a nervously shaking voice. "Don't you know that snakes climb trees?"

"Nonsense," retorted Sahwah. "Whoever heard of a snake climbing a tree?"

An argument started below, several voices upholding each side, some maintaining emphatically that snakes did climb trees; others holding out quite as determinedly that they didn't.

"Anyway, *this* one might," concluded the one who had started the argument, in a triumphant tone.

"What are we going to do?" someone asked Miss Judy.

"I'll get father to come and shoot it," replied Miss Judy.

Just then there came an excited shriek from Sahwah. "It's coming out! I see the bushes moving."

The girls scattered in all directions; Miss Peckham, up on her rock, covered her ears with her hands, as though there was going to be an explosion.

"Here it comes!"

Sahwah, leaning low over her branch, nearly fell out of the tree in her excitement, as her eye caught the gleam of red and black among the bushes. Miss Judy scrambled up on the rock beside Miss Peckham.

There was a violent agitation of the ferns and bushes underneath Ponemah, a sort of scrambling movement, accompanied by a muffled squeaking, and then a truly remarkable creature bounced into view - a creature whose body consisted of a long stocking, red and black in alternate stripes, in the toe of which some live animal frantically squeaked and struggled, leaping almost a foot from the ground in its efforts to escape from its prison, and dragging the gaudy striped length behind it through a series of thrillingly lifelike wriggles.

"Hi!" called Sahwah with a great shout of laughter. "It's nothing but a stocking with something in it."

In reaction from her former alarm Miss Judy laughed until she fell off the rock, and sat helplessly on the ground watching the frantic struggles of the creature in the stocking to free itself. Hearing the laughter, those who had fled at the first alarm came hastening back, and all promptly went into hysterics when they saw the stocking writhing on the ground, and all were equally as helpless as Miss Judy and Sahwah.

"Only Tiny Armstrong's stocking!" gasped Miss Judy, wiping away her tears of merriment with her middy sleeve. "I told her they would cause a riot in camp!"

Only Miss Peckham did not laugh; she looked crossly around at the desperately amused girls.

"Oh, Miss Peckham," gurgled Bengal, "you said it reared up and menaced you with its great, wicked h-head! You said its hood was swelled up with ferocity and venom, and it hissed sibilantly at you."

Bengal rolled over and over on the ground, shrieking

with mirth.

Miss Peckham, her face a dull red, moved off in the direction of the tent.

Others came up, excitedly demanding to know what the joke was.

"She thought it was a coral snake, and it was Tiny's stocking," giggled Bengal, going into a fresh spasm.

"Well, what if I did?" remarked Miss Peckham, turning around and looking at her frigidly. "It's a mistake anybody could easily make, I'm sure." And she went stiffly up into the tent.

Sahwah and Miss Judy had somewhat recovered their composure by this time, and having captured the wildly agitated stocking they released from it a half-grown chipmunk, who, beside himself with fright and bewilderment, dashed away into the woods like a flash.

"How frightened he was, poor little fellow!" cried Migwan compassionately. "It wasn't any joke for *him*. He must have been nearly frantic in there. How do you suppose he ever got in?"

"Walked in, or fell in, possibly," replied Miss Judy, "and then couldn't find his way out again. Tiny had those modest little stockings of hers hanging on the tent ropes this morning, and it was easy enough for a chipmunk to get in."

Carrying the stocking between them, and followed by all the girls who had been standing around, Sahwah and Miss Judy started for Bedlam to tell Tiny about the panic her hosiery had caused, but halfway to Bedlam the trumpet sounded for dinner and the deputation broke up in a wild rush for the bungalow. Miss Peckham carefully avoided Miss Judy's eye all through dinner.

When the Winnebagos sauntered back to their tents for rest hour they all found large, wafer-sealed envelopes lying in conspicuous places upon their respective tables. Sahwah pounced upon the one in Gitchee-Gummee and looked at it curiously. On it was written in large red letters:

TO THE DWELLERS IN GITCHEE-GUMMEE

IMPORTANT!!!

"Whatever can this be?" she asked in mystified tones. Miss Judy was not in the tent.

"Open it," commanded Agony.

Sahwah slit the envelope with the knife that she always kept hanging at her belt, and pulled out a sheet of rough, brown paper, on which was drawn the picture of a girl bound fast to a tree by ropes that went round and round her body, while a band of Indians danced a savage war dance around her. Underneath was printed in the same large red letters as those which adorned the outside of the envelope:

BE DOWN ON THE DOCK AT SUNDOWN
WITHOUT FAIL PREPARED TO UNDERGO
THE ORDEAL WHICH ALL
DWELLERS IN THE ALLEY MUST
SUFFER BEFORE BEING WELCOMED
INTO THE INNER
CIRCLE OF ALLEY
SPIRITS.

WARNING: MENTION NOT THIS SUMMONS
TO A LIVING SOUL OR AWFUL
WILL BE THE CONSEQUENCES.

SIGNED: THE TERRIBLE TWELVE.
P.S. BRING YOUR BATHING SUITS.

"What on earth?" cried Hinpoha in bewilderment.

"It's the Alley Initiation!" exclaimed Sahwah. "I heard someone asking when it was going to be. Mary Sylvester and Jo Severance and several more of the old girls were talking about it while they were in the water today. It seems that the girls who have lived in the Alley before always hold an initiation for the new girls before they let them in on their larks."

"I wonder what they're going to do to us," mused Hinpoha. "That advice to bring your bathing suit sounds suspicious to me."

"Do you suppose they're going to throw us into the river?" asked Agony.

"Nonsense," replied Sahwah. "Half the new girls in the Alley can't swim. Dr. Grayson wouldn't allow it, anyway. He made a girl come out of the water during swimming hour this morning for trying to duck another girl. They'll just make us ridiculous, that's all."

"Well, whatever they ask us to do, let's not make a fuss," said Hinpoha. "Here comes Miss Judy. Put that letter out of sight and act perfectly unconcerned."

Sahwah whipped the envelope into her suitcase and flung herself down on her bed; the others followed her example; and when a moment later Miss Judy stepped into the tent and looked quizzically at the trio she found them apparently wrapped in placid slumber.

Shortly before seven that evening, when the Avenue girls were dancing in the bungalow, Sahwah and Hinpoha and Agony quietly detached themselves from the group and slipped down to the dock to find Katherine and Oh-Pshaw and Jean Lawrence already down there, swinging their feet over the end of the pier and waiting for something to happen. Down the hillside other forms were stealing; Migwan, and Gladys, and Bengal Virden, followed by Tiny Armstrong, until practically all the inhabitants of the Alley were gathered upon the dock. Miss Judy was leaning over the edge of the pier untying the launch.

The neophytes watched intently every move that the old girls made, and were somewhat reassured when they saw that they had brought their bathing suits, too.

"Are all assembled?" asked Miss Judy, straightening up and looking over her shoulder inquiringly.

"Not yet," answered Mary Sylvester, taking an inventory of girls present.

"Who isn't here yet?"

"Carmen Chadwick and the Lone Wolf. Oh, they're coming now, so is Miss Amesbury."

Migwan felt a little flustered as Miss Amesbury came smiling into their midst. She didn't in the least mind being initiated, but she did rather hate to have Miss Amesbury see her made ridiculous. She would much rather not have her looking on.

Carmen Chadwick looked quite pale and scared as she joined the group on the dock, and took hold of Katherine's arm as if to seek her protection.

"All ready now?" asked Miss Judy.

"Ay, ay, skipper," replied Tiny Armstrong.

"Man the boat!" commanded Miss Judy.

The girls got into the launch and Miss Judy started the engine. They rode a short distance up the river to the Whaleback, a small island shaped, as its name indicated, like a whale's back.

It was quite flat, only slightly elevated above the surface of the water. On one side it had rather a wide beach covered with stones and littered with driftwood; behind this beach rose a dense growth of pines that extended down to the very edge of the water on the other side of the island.

The initiation party disembarked upon the beach. A huge fire was laid ready and Miss Judy lit it, then she requested the new girls to sit down in a place which she designated at one side of it, while the old girls seated themselves in a row opposite. Sahwah took note that the new girls were in the full glare of the firelight, while the old ones sat in the shadow.

Miss Judy opened the ceremonies. Stepping into the light, she addressed the neophytes. "Since the dwellers in the Alley live together in such intimate companionship it is necessary that all be properly introduced to each other, so that we shall never mistake our own. We shall now proceed with the introductions. As soon as a new girl or councilor recognizes herself in the pictures we shall proceed to draw, let her come forward and bow to the ground three times in acknowledgment, uttering the words, 'Behold, it is I! who else *could* it be?'"

She poked up the fire to a brighter blaze and then sat down beside Tiny Armstrong on the end of a log. As she seated herself Jo Severance rose and came forward demurely. Jo was an accomplished elocutionist, and a born mimic. Assuming a timid, shrinking demeanor, and speaking in a high, shrill voice, she piped,

> "Mother, may I go out to swim?"
> "Yes, my darling daughter,
> Put on your nice new bathing suit,
> But don't go near the water!"

"Don't you think it's unladylike to have your muscles all hard and developed?"

Oh-Pshaw buried her face in her handkerchief with a convulsive giggle. The voice, the intonation, the expression, were Carmen Chadwick to a T. But how did the Alleys know about her attitude toward bathing? She had not told anyone. Then she recalled that the Lone Wolf had walked behind them on the pier that morning when Carmen had been talking to her. Had the Lone Wolf also heard them talking about her? Agony wondered in a sudden rush of embarrassment.

There was no mistaking the first "portrait." All eyes were focused upon Carmen, and blushing and shrinking she went forward to make the required acknowledgment.

"Beh-hold, it is I; w-who else could it be?" she faltered, and it sounded so irresistibly funny that the listeners went into spasms of mirth.

Carmen crept back to her place and hid her face in Katherine's lap while Jo Severance passed on to the next "portrait." Climbing up an enormous tree stump, she flung out her arms and began to shriek wildly, waving back an imaginary group of girls. Then she proclaimed in important tones: "It had broad, alternating rings of black and red, the distinguishing marks of the coral snake, one of the seventeen poisonous reptiles out of the one hundred and eleven species of snakes found in the United States. It reared up and menaced me with its great, wicked -"

The remainder of her speech was lost in the great roar of laughter that went up from old and new girls alike.

Miss Peckham turned fiery red, and looked angrily from Jo Severance to Miss Judy, but there was no help for it; she had to go forward and claim the portrait.

"Behold, it is I; who else *could* it be?" she snapped, and the mirth broke out louder than before. The "who else *could* it be?" was so like Miss Peckham.

One by one the other candidates were shown their portraits, that is, as many as had displayed any conspicuous peculiarities

"O Pom-pom! O dear Pom-pom, O *darling* Pom-pom!" gushed Jo, rolling her eyes in ecstasy, and Bengal Virden, laughing sheepishly, went forward.

Miss Amesbury watched the performance with tears of merriment rolling down her cheeks. "I never saw anything so funny!" she exclaimed to Mary Sylvester. "That phrase, 'who else *could* it be' is a perfect gem."

Agony was somewhat disappointed that her portrait was not painted; it would have drawn her into more notice. So far she was only "among those present" at camp. None of the old girls had paid any attention to her.

After all the portraits had been painted the rest of the girls were called upon to do individual stunts. Some sang, some made speeches, some danced, and the worse the performance the greater the applause from the initiators. One slender, dark-eyed girl with short hair whistled, with two fingers in her mouth. At the first note Migwan and Gladys started and clasped each other's hands. The mystery of the fairy piping they had heard in the woods that first afternoon was solved. The same clear, sweet notes came thrilling out between her fingers, alluring as the pipes of Pan. The whistler was a girl named Noel Carrington; she was one of the younger girls whom nobody had noticed particularly before. Her whistling brought wild applause which was perfectly sincere; her performance delighted the audience beyond measure. She was called back again and again until at last, quite out of breath, she begged for mercy, when she was allowed to retire on the condition that she would whistle some more as soon as she got her breath back.

Noel's performance closed the stunts. When she had sat down

Miss Judy rose and said that she guessed the Alley dwellers were pretty well acquainted with each other, and would now go for a swim in the moonlight. Soon all but Carmen Chadwick were splashing in the silvery water, playing hide and seek with the moonbeams on the ripples and feeling a thrill and a magic in the river which was never there in the daylight. After a glorious frolic they came out to stand around the fire and eat marshmallows until it was time to go back to camp.

"Initiation wasn't so terrible after all," Carmen confided to Katherine in the launch.

"Heaps of fun," replied Katherine, laughing reminiscently.

"Isn't Miss Peckham a prune?" whispered Sybil's voice behind Katherine. "I'm glad she's not my councilor."

"She's mine, worse luck," answered Bengal Virden's voice dolefully.

"Too bad," whispered Sybil feelingly.

The launch came up alongside the dock just as the first bugle was blowing, and the Alley, old girls arm in arm with the new, went straight up to bed.

CHAPTER V

ON THE ROAD FROM ATLANTIS

"Would you like to come along?"

Agony, sitting alone on the pier, idly watching the river as it flowed endlessly around its great curve, looked up to see Mary Sylvester standing beside her. It was just after quiet hour and the rest of the camp had gone on the regular Wednesday afternoon trip to the village to buy picture postcards and elastic and Kodak films and all the various small wares which girls in camp are in constant need of; and also to regale themselves on ice-cream cones and root beer, the latter a traditionally favorite refreshment of the Camp Keewaydin girls, being a special home product of Mrs. Bayne, who kept the "trading post."

Agony had not joined the expedition this afternoon, because she needed nothing in the way of supplies, and for once had no craving for root beer, while she did want to finish a letter to her father that she had commenced during rest hour. But the hilarity of the others as they piled into the canoes to be towed up the river by the launch lured her down to the dock to see them off - Miss Judy standing at the wheel of the launch and Tiny Armstrong in the stern of the last canoe, as the head and tail of the procession respectively. Beside Miss Judy in the launch were all the Minnows, gazing longingly back at the ones who were allowed to tow in the canoes. Only those who had taken the swimming test might go into the canoes - towing or paddling or at any other time; this rule of the camp was as inviolable as the laws of the Medes and the Persians. And of those who could swim, only the Sharks might take out a canoe without a councilor, and this privilege was also denied the Sharks if they failed to demonstrate their ability to handle a canoe skilfully.

Sahwah and Hinpoha were among the new girls who had qualified for the canoe privilege during the very first week; also Undine Girelle. The other Winnebagos had to content themselves thus far with the privilege of towing or paddling in a canoe that was in charge of a councilor or a qualified Water Witch; all except Oh-Pshaw, who had to ride in the launch.

Agony looked at Oh-Pshaw standing beside Miss Judy at the wheel, laughing with her at some joke; at Sahwah and Undine sitting together in the canoe right behind the launch, leaning luxuriously back against their paddles, which they were using as back rests; heard Jean Lawrence's infectious laugh floating back on the breeze; and she began to regret that she had stayed at home. She found she was no longer in the mood to finish her letter; she lingered on the pier after the floating caravan had disappeared from view behind the trees on Whaleback.

She looked up in surprise at the sound of Mary Sylvester's voice coming from behind her on the dock.

"I thought you had gone to the village with the others," she said. "I was almost sure I saw you in the boat with Pom-pom."

"No, I didn't go, you see," replied Mary. "I am going off on an expedition of my own this afternoon. The woman who took care of me as a child lives not far from here in a little village called Atlantis - classic name! Mother asked me to look her up, and Mrs. Grayson gave me permission to go over this afternoon. I'm going to row across the river to that landing place where we got out the other night, leave the boat in the bushes, and then follow the path through the woods. It's about six miles to Atlantis - would you care to walk that far? It would be twelve miles there and back, you know. I'm just ripe for a long hike today, it's so cool and clear, but it's not nearly so pleasant going alone as it would be to have someone along to talk to on the way. Wouldn't you like to come along and keep me company? I can easily get permission from Mrs. Grayson for you."

Agony was a trifle daunted at the thought of walking twelve miles in one afternoon, but was so overwhelmed with secret gratification that the prominent Mary Sylvester had invited her that she never once thought of refusing.

"I'd love to go," she exclaimed animatedly, jumping up with alacrity. "I was beginning to feel a wee bit bored sitting here doing nothing; I feel ripe for a long hike myself."

"I'm so glad you do!" replied Mary Sylvester, with the utmost cordiality. "Come on with me until I tell Mrs. Grayson that you are coming with me."

Mrs. Grayson readily gave her permission for Agony to go with Mary. There was very little that Mrs. Grayson would have refused Mary Sylvester, so high did this clear-eyed girl stand in the regard of all Camp directors, from the Doctor down. Mary was one of the few girls allowed to go away from camp without a councilor; in fact, she sometimes acted as councilor to the younger girls when a trip had to be made and no councilor was free. Mrs. Grayson would willingly have trusted any girl to Mary's care - or the whole camp, for that matter, should occasion arise, knowing that her good sense and judgment could be relied upon. So Agony, under Mary's wing, received the permission that otherwise would not have been given her.

"Yes, it will be all right for you to go in your bloomers," said Mrs. Grayson, in answer to Agony's question on the subject. "Our girls always wear them to the villages about here; the people are accustomed to seeing them. That green bloomer suit of yours is very pretty, Agony," she added, "even prettier than our regulation blue ones."

"I spilled syrup on my regular blue ones," replied Agony, "and had to wash them out this morning; that's why I'm wearing these green ones. Do you mind if I break up the camp color scheme for one day?"

"Not at all, under the circumstances," replied Mrs. Grayson, with a smile. "If it's going to be a choice of green bloomers or none at all -" She waved the laughing girls away and returned to the knotty problem in accounts she had been working on when interrupted.

"Isn't she lovely?" exclaimed Mary enthusiastically, as they came out of the bungalow and walked along the Alley path toward Gitchee-Gummee to get Agony's hat. "She has such a way of trusting us girls that we just couldn't disappoint her."

"She is lovely," echoed Agony, as they went up the steps of Gitchee-Gummee.

"I think I'll leave a note for the girls telling them I won't be back at supper time," said Agony, hastily pulling out her tablet. "They will be wondering what has become of me."

It gave her no small thrill of pleasure to write that note and tuck it under Hinpoha's hairbrush on the table: "Gone on a long hike with Mary Sylvester; won't be back until bed time." How delightfully important and prominent that sounded! The others admired Mary, too, but none of them had been invited to go on a long hike with her. She, Agony, was being drawn into that intimate inner circle of the Alley dwellers to which she had hitherto aspired in vain.

They were soon across the river, with the boat fastened in the bushes, and, leaving the shore, struck straight into the woods, following a path that curved and twisted, but carried them ever toward the north, in the direction where Atlantis lay. The way was cool and shady, the whiff of the pines invigorating, and the distance uncoiled rapidly beneath the feet of the two girls as they fared on with vigorous, springy footsteps along the

Hildegard G. Frey

pleasant way. Ferns and wild flowers bordered the path; there were brilliant cardinal flowers, pale forget-me-nots, slender blossomed blue vervain, cheerful red lilies. In places where the woods were so thick that the sun never penetrated, great logs lay about completely covered with moss, looking like sofas upholstered in green, while the round stones scattered about everywhere looked like hassocks and footstools which belonged to the same set as the green sofas.

Once Mary stopped and crushed something under her foot, something white that grew up beside the path.

"What was that?" asked Agony curiously.

"Deadly amanita," replied Mary. "It's a toadstool - a poisonous one."

"How can you tell a poisonous toadstool from a harmless one?" asked Agony. "They all look alike to me."

"A poisonous one has a ring around the stem, and it grows up out of a 'poison cup,'" explained Mary. "See, here are some more."

Agony drew back as Mary pointed out another clump of the pale spores, innocent enough looking in their resemblance to the edible mushroom, but base villians at heart; veritable Borgias of the woods.

"Aren't you afraid to touch it?" asked Agony, as Mary tilted over a sickly looking head and indicated the identifying ring and the poison cup.

"No danger," replied Mary. "They're only poisonous if you eat them."

"You know a great deal about the woods, don't you?" Agony said respectfully.

"I ought to," replied Mary. "I've camped in the woods for five summers. You can't help finding out a few things, you know, even if you're as stupid as I."

"You're not stupid!" said Agony emphatically, glad of the opportunity to pay a compliment. "I'm the stupid one about things like that. I never could remember all those things you call woodcraft. I declare, I've forgotten already whether it's the poisonous ones that have the rings, or the other kind."

Mary laughed and stood unconcernedly while a small snake ran over her foot. "It's a good thing Miss Peckham isn't here," she remarked. "Did you ever see anything so funny as that coral snake business of hers?" she added, laughing good naturedly. "Poor Miss Peckham won't be allowed to forget that episode all summer. It's too bad she resents it so. She could get no end of fun out of it if she could only see the funny side."

"Yes, it's too bad," agreed Agony. "The more she resents it the more the girls will tease her about it."

"I'm sorry for her," continued Mary. "She's never had any experience being a councilor and it's all new to her. She's never been teased before. She'll soon see that it happens to everybody else, too, and then she'll feel differently about it. Look at the way everybody makes fun of Tiny Armstrong's blanket, and her red bathing suit, and her gaudy stockings; but she never gets cross about it. Tiny's a wonder," she added enthusiastically. "Did you see her demonstrating the Australian Crawl yesterday in swimming hour? She has a stroke like the propeller of a boat. I never saw anything so powerful."

"If Tiny ever assaulted anyone in earnest there wouldn't be anything left of them," said Agony. "She's a regular Amazon. They ought to call her Hypolita instead of Tiny."

"And yet, she's just as gentle as she is powerful," replied Mary. "She wouldn't hurt a fly if she could help it. Neither would she do anything mean to anybody, or show partiality in the swimming tests. She's absolutely fair and square; that's why all the girls accept her decisions without a complaint, even when they're disappointed. Everybody says she is the best swimming teacher they've ever had here at camp. Once they had an instructor who had a special liking for a certain girl who couldn't manage to learn to swim, and because that girl was wild to go in a canoe on one of the trips the instructor pretended that she had given her an individual test on the afternoon before the trip, and told Mrs. Grayson the girl had passed it. The girl was allowed to go in a canoe and on the trip it upset and she was very nearly drowned before the others realized that she could not swim. Tiny isn't like that," she continued. "She would lose her best friend rather than tell a lie to get her a favor that she didn't deserve. I hate cheats!" she burst out vehemently, her fine eyes flashing. "If girls can't win honors fairly they ought to go without them."

This random conversation upon one and another of the phases of camp life, illustrating as it did Mary's rigid code of honor, was destined to recur many times to Agony in the weeks that followed, with a poignant force that etched every one of Mary's speeches ineradicably upon her brain. Just now it was nothing more to her than small talk to which she replied in kind.

They stopped after a bit to drink from a clear spring that bubbled up in the path, and sat down to rest awhile under a huge tree. Mary leaned her head back against the trunk and drawing a small book from her sweater pocket she opened it upon her knee.

"What is the book?" asked Agony.

"*The Desert Garden*, by Edwin Langham," replied Mary.

"Oh, do you know *The Desert Garden?*" cried Agony in delighted wonder. "I've actually lived on that book for the last two years. I'm wild about Edwin Langham. I've read every word he's ever written. Have you read *The Silent Years?*"

Mary nodded.

"*The Lost Chord*? I think that's the most wonderful book I've ever read, that and *The Desert Garden*. If I could ever see and speak to Edwin Langham I should die from happiness. I've never felt that way about any other author. When I read his books I feel reverent somehow, as if I were in church, although there isn't a word of religion in them. The things he writes are so fine and true and noble; he must be that way himself. Do you remember that part about the bird in *The Desert Garden*, the bird with the broken wing, that would never fly again, singing to the lame man who would never walk? And the flower that was so determined to blossom that it grew in the desert and bloomed there?"

"Yes," answered Mary, "it was very beautiful."

"It's the most beautiful thing that was ever written!" declared Agony enthusiastically. "It would be the greatest joy of my life to see the man who wrote those books."

"Maybe you will, some day," said Mary, rising from her mossy seat and preparing to take the path again.

It was not long after that that they came to the edge of the woods, and saw before them the scattered houses of the little village of Atlantis. Mary's old nurse was overjoyed to see her, and pressed the two girls to stay and eat big soft ginger cookies on the shady back porch, and quench their thirst with glasses of cool milk, while she inquired minutely after the health of Mary's "ma" and "pa."

"Mrs. Simmons is the best old nurse that ever was," said Mary to Agony, as they took their way back to the woods an hour later. "I'm so glad to have had this opportunity of paying her a visit. I haven't seen her for nearly ten years. Wasn't she funny, though, when I told her that father might have to go to Japan in the interests of his firm? She thought there was nobody in Japan but heathens and missionaries."

"Shall you go to Japan too, if your father goes?" asked Agony.

"I most likely shall," replied Mary. "I finished my school this June and do not intend to go to college for another year anyway; so I might as well have the trip and the experience of living in a foreign country. Father would only have to remain there one year, or two at the most."

"How soon are you going?" asked Agony, a little awed by Mary's casual tone as she spoke of the great journey. Evidently Mary had traveled much, for the prospect of going around the world did not seem to excite her in the least.

They were sitting in Mrs. Simmons' little spring house when Mary told about the possibility of her going to Japan. This spring house stood at some distance from the house; down at the point where the lane ran off from the main road. It looked so utterly cool and inviting, with its vine covered walls, that with an exclamation of pleasure the two girls turned aside for one more drink before beginning the long walk through the woods.

Seated upon the edge of the basin which held the water, Mary talked of Japan, and Agony wheeled around upon the narrow ledge to gaze at her in wonder and envy.

"I wish *I* could go to Japan!" she exclaimed vehemently, giving a vigorous kick with her foot to express her longing. The motion disturbed her balance and she careened over sidewise; Mary put out her hand to steady her, lost *her* balance, and went with a splash into the basin. The water was not deep, but it was very, very wet, and Mary came out dripping.

For a moment the two girls stood helpless with laughter; then Mary said: "I suppose I'll have to go back and get some dry things from Mrs. Simmons, but I wish I didn't; it will take us quite a while to go back, and it will delay us considerably. I promised Mrs. Grayson I'd be back in camp before dark, and we won't be able to make it if we go back to Mrs. Simmons's.

I've a good mind to go on just as I am; it's so hot I can't possibly take cold."

"I tell you what we can do," said Agony, getting a sudden inspiration. "We can divide these bloomers of mine in half. They're made on a foundation of thinner material that will do very well for me to wear home, and you can wear the green part. With your sweater on over them nobody will ever know whether you have on a middy or not. We can carry your wet suit on a pole through the woods and it'll be dry by the time we get home, and you won't have to lose any time by going back to Mrs. Simmons's."

"Great idea!" said Mary, brightening. "Are you really willing to divide your bloomers? I'd be ever so much obliged."

"It's no trouble," replied Agony. "All I have to do is cut the threads where the top is tacked on to the foundation. It's really two pairs of bloomers." She was already cutting the tacking threads with her pocket knife.

Mary put on the green bloomers and Agony the brown foundation pair, and laughing over the mishap and the clever way of handling the problem, the two crossed the road and entered the woods.

"What's that loud cheeping noise?" Agony asked almost as soon as they had entered into the deep shadow of the high pines.

"Sounds like a bird in trouble," answered Mary, her practised ear recognizing the note of distress in the incessant twittering.

A few steps farther they came upon a man sitting in a wheel chair under one of the tallest pines they had ever seen, a man whose right foot was so thickly wrapped in bandages that it was three times the size of the other one. He was peering intently up into the tree above him, and did not notice the approach of the two girls. Mary and Agony followed his gaze and saw, high up among the topmost swaying branches, a sight that thrilled them with pity and distress. Dangling by a string which was tangled about one of her feet, hung a mother robin, desperately struggling to get free, fluttering, fluttering, beating the air frantically with her wings and uttering piercing cries of anguish that drove the hearers almost to desperation. Nearby was her nest, and on the edge of it sat the mate, uttering cries as shrill with anguish as those of the helpless captive.

"Oh, the poor, poor bird!" cried Mary, her eyes filling with tears of pity and grief. At the sound of her voice the man in the wheel chair lowered his eyes and became aware of the girls' presence. As he turned to look at them Mary caught in his eyes a look of infinite horror and pity at the plight of the wretched bird above him. That expression deepened Mary's emotion; the tears began to run down her cheeks. Agony stood beside her stricken and silent.

"How did it happen?" Mary asked huskily, addressing the stranger unceremoniously.

"I don't know exactly," replied the man. "I was sitting here reading when all of a sudden I heard the bird's shrill cry of distress and looked up to see her dangling there at the end of that string."

"Can't we do something?" asked Mary, putting her hands over her ears to shut out the piercing cries. "She'll flutter herself to death before long."

"I'm afraid she will," replied the man, "There doesn't seem to be any hope of her freeing herself."

"She shan't flutter herself to death," said Mary, with sudden resolution. "I'm going to climb the tree and cut her loose."

"That will be impossible," said the man. "She is up in the very top of the tree."

"I'm going to try, anyway," replied Mary, with spirit. "Let me take your knife, will you please, Agony?"

The lowest branches of the pine were far above her head, and in order to get a foothold in them Mary had to climb a neighboring tree and swing herself across. The ground seemed terrifying far away even from this lowest branch; but this was only the beginning. She resolutely refrained from looking down and kept on steadily, branch above branch, until she reached the one from which the robin hung. Then began the most perilous part of the undertaking. To reach the bird she must crawl out on this branch for a distance of at least six feet, there being no limb directly underneath for her to walk out on. Praying for a steady balance, she swung herself astride of the branch, and holding on tightly with her hands began hitching herself slowly outward. The bough bent sickeningly under her; Agony below shrieked and covered her eyes; then opened them again and continued to gaze in horrified fascination as inch by inch Mary neared the wildly fluttering bird, whose terror had increased a hundred-fold at the human presence so near it.

There came an ominous cracking sound; Agony uttered another shriek and turned away; the next instant the shrill cries of the bird ceased; the man in the chair gave vent to a long drawn "Ah-h!" Agony looked up to see the exhausted bird fluttering to the ground beside her, a length of string still hanging to its foot, while Mary slowly and carefully worked her way back to the trunk of the tree. In a few minutes she slid to the ground and sat there, breathless and trembling, but triumphant.

"I got it!" she panted. Then, turning to the man in the chair, she exclaimed, "There now, who said it was impossible?"

The man applauded vigorously. "That was the bravest act I have ever seen performed," he said admiringly. "You're the right stuff, whoever you are, and I take my hat off to you."

Hildegard G. Frey

"Anybody would have done it," murmured Mary modestly, as she rose and prepared to depart.

"How could you do it?" marveled Agony, as the two walked homeward through the woods. "Weren't you horribly scared?"

"Yes, I was," admitted Mary frankly. "When I started to go out on that branch I was shaking so that I could hardly hold on. It seemed miles to the ground, and I got so dizzy I turned faint for a moment. But I tried to think of something else, and kept on going, and pretty soon I could reach the string to cut it."

The boundless admiration with which Agony regarded Mary's act of bravery was gradually swallowed up in envy. Why hadn't she herself been the one to climb up and rescue that poor bird? She would give anything to have done such a spectacular thing. Deep in her heart, however, she knew she would never have had the courage to crawl out on that branch even if she had thought of it first.

Silence fell upon the two girls as they walked along in the gradually failing light; all topics of conversation seemed to have been exhausted. Mary's clothes were dry before they were through the woods, and she put them on to save the trouble of carrying them, giving Agony back her green bloomers.

"Thank you so much for letting me wear them," she said earnestly. "If it hadn t been for your doing that I wouldn t have been in time to save that robin. It was really that inspiration of yours that saved him, not my climbing the tree.'

Even in the hour of her triumph Mary was eager to give the credit to someone else, and Agony began to feel rather humble and small before such a generous spirit, even though her vanity strove to accept the measure of credit given as justly due.

When they were crossing the river they saw Dr. Grayson standing on the dock, shading his eyes to look over the water.

"There's the Doctor, looking for us!" exclaimed Mary. "It must be late and he's worried about us." She doubled her speed with the oars, hailing the Doctor across the water to reassure him. A few moments later the boat touched the dock.

"Mary," said the Doctor, before she was fairly out, "a message has come from your father saying that he must sail for Japan one week from today and you must come home immediately. In order to catch the boat you will have to leave for San Francisco not later than the day after tomorrow. There is an early train for New York tomorrow morning from Green's Landing. I will take you down in the launch, for the river steamer will not get there in time. Be ready to leave camp at half past five tomorrow morning. You will have to pack tonight."

Mary gasped and clutched Agony's hand convulsively.

"I have - to - leave - camp!" she breathed faintly. "I'm - going - to - Japan!"

CHAPTER VI

A CAMP HEROINE

Mary Sylvester was gone. Sung to and wept over by her friends and admirers, who had risen at dawn to see her off, she had departed with Dr. Grayson in the camp launch just as the sun was beginning to gild the ripples on the surface of the river. She left behind her many grief stricken hearts.

"Camp won't be camp without Mary!" Bengal Virden had sobbed, trickling tearfully back to Ponemah with a long tress of black hair clutched tightly in her hand - a souvenir which she had begged from Mary at the moment of parting. Next to Pom-pom, Mary Sylvester was Bengal's greatest crush. "I'm going to put it under my pillow and sleep on it every night," Bengal had sniffed tearfully, displaying the tress to her tentmates.

"What utter nonsense!" Miss Peckham had remarked with a contemptuous sniff. Miss Peckham considered the fuss they were making over Mary's departure perfectly ridiculous, and was decidely cross because Bengal had awakened her with her lamenting before the bugle blew.

Migwan and Gladys, on the other hand, remembering their own early "crushes," managed not to smile at Bengal's sentimental foolishness about the lock of hair, and Gladys gravely gave her a hand-painted envelope to keep the precious tress in.

Completely tired out by the long tramp of the day before, Agony did not waken in time to see Mary off, and when the second bugle finally brought her to consciousness she discovered that she had a severe headache and did not want any breakfast. Miss Judy promptly bore her off to the "Infirmary," a tent set off by itself away from the noises of camp, and left her there to stay quietly by herself. In the quiet atmosphere of the "Infirmary" she soon fell asleep again, to waken at times, listen to the singing of the birds in the woods, feel the breezes stealing caressingly through her hair, and then to drop back once more into blissful drowsiness which erased from her mind all memory of yesterday's visit to Atlantis, and of Mary Sylvester's wonderful rescue of the robin. As yet no word of Mary's heroism had reached the ears of the camp; she had departed without the mead of praise that was due her.

Councilors and all felt depressed over Mary's untimely departure, especially Miss Judy, Tiny Armstrong and the Lone Wolf, with whom she had been particularly intimate, and with these three leading spirits cast down gloom was thick everywhere. Morning Sing went flat - the high tenors couldn't keep in tune without Mary to lead them, and nobody else could make the gestures for The Lone Fish Ball. It seemed strange, too, to see Dr. Grayson's chair empty, and to do without his jolly morning talk. Everyone who had gotten up early was full of yawns and out of sorts.

"What's the matter with everybody?" asked Katherine of Jean Lawrence, as they cleaned up Bedlam for tent inspection. "Camp looks like a funeral."

Jean's dimples were nowhere in evidence and her face looked unnaturally solemn as she bent over her bed to straighten the blankets.

"It feels like one, too," replied Jean, still grave. "With Bengal crying all over the place and Miss Judy looking so cut up it's enough to dampen everybody's spirits."

Hildegard G. Frey

Talk lapsed between the two and each went on cleaning up her side of the tent. A moment later, however, Jean's dimples came back again when she came upon Katherine's toothbrush in one of her tennis shoes. That toothbrush had disappeared two days before and the tent had been turned upside down in a vain search for it.

Katherine pounced upon the truant toilet article gleefully. "Look in your other shoe," she begged Jean, "and see if you can find my fountain pen. That's missing too."

Jean obligingly shook out her shoe, but no pen came to light.

"There's something dark in the bottom of the water pitcher," announced Oh-Pshaw, who was setting the toilet table to rights. "Maybe that's it."

She bared her arm to the elbow and plunged it into the water, but withdrew it immediately with a shriek that caused Katherine and Jean to drop their bed-making in alarm.

"What's the matter?" asked Katherine.

"It's an animal, a horrid, dead animal!" Oh-Pshaw gasped shudderingly, backing precipitously away from the water pitcher. "It's furry, and soft, and - ugh! stiff!"

"What is it?" demanded Katherine, peering curiously into the pitcher, in whose slightly turbid depths she could see a dark object lying.

"Don't touch it!" begged Oh-Pshaw, as Katherine's hand went down into the water.

"Nonsense," scoffed Katherine, "a dead creature can't hurt you. See, it's only a little mouse that fell into the pitcher and got drowned. Poor little mousy, it's a shame he had to meet such a sad fate when he came to visit us."

"Katherine Adams, put that mouse away!" cried Oh-Pshaw, getting around behind the bed. "How can you bear to touch such a thing?"

"Doesn't he look pathetic, with his little paws held out that way?" continued Katherine, unmoved by Oh-Pshaw's expression of terrified disgust. "I don't doubt but what he was the father of a large family - or maybe the mother - and there will be great sorrow in the nest out in the field when he doesn't come home to supper."

"Throw it away!" commanded Oh-Pshaw.

"Let's have a funeral," suggested Jean. "Here, we can lay him out in the lid of my writing paper box."

"Grand idea," replied Katherine, carefully depositing the deceased on the floor beside her bed.

A few minutes later the Lone Wolf, coming along to inspect the tent, found a black middy tie hanging from the tent post, surmounted by a wreath of field daisies, while inside the mouse was laid out in state in the lid of Jean's writing paper box, surrounded by flowers and leaves.

Word of the tragedy that had taken place in Bedlam was all over camp in no time, and crowds came to gaze on the face of the departed one. A special edition of the camp paper was gotten out, with monstrous headlines, giving the details of the accident, and announcing the funeral for three o'clock.

Dr. Grayson returned to camp early in the afternoon, bringing with him a professor friend whom he had invited to spend the week-end at camp. As the two men stepped from the launch to the landing a sound of wailing greeted their ears; long drawn out moans, heartbroken sobs, despairing shrieks, blood-curdling cries.

Hildegard G. Frey

"What can be the matter?" gasped the Doctor in consternation.

He raced up the path to the bungalow and stood frozen to the spot by the sight that greeted his eyes. Down the Alley came a procession headed by a wheelbarrow filled with field daisies and wild red lilies, all arranged around a pasteboard box in the center; behind the wheelbarrow came two girls with black middy ties around their heads, carrying spades in their hands; behind them marched, two and two, all the girls who lived in the Alley, each with a black square over her face and all wailing and sobbing and shrieking at the top of their voices. The procession came to a halt in front of the bungalow porch and Katherine Adams detached herself from the ranks. Mounting a rock, she broke out into an impassioned funeral oration that put Mark Anthony's considerably in the shade. She was waving her hands in an extravagant gesture to accompany an especially eloquent passage, when she suddenly caught sight of Dr. Grayson standing watching the proceedings.

The mourners saw her suddenly stand as if petrified, the gesture frozen in mid air, the word on her lips chopped off in the middle as with a knife. Following her startled glance the others also saw Dr. Grayson and the visitor. An indescribable sound rose from the funeral train; the transition noise of anguished wailing turning into uncontrollable laughter; then such a shout went up that the birds dozing in the trees overhead flew out in startled circles and went darting away with loud squawks of alarm.

"Go on, go on," urged Dr. Grayson, with twinkling eyes, "don't let me interrupt the flow of eloquence."

But Katherine, abashed and tongue-tied in his presence always, could not utter another word, and, blushing furiously, slid down off the rock and took refuge behind the daisy-covered bier. The procession, agitated by great waves of laughter, moved on toward the woods, where the mouse was duly interred with solemn ceremonies.

"Will your father think I'm dreadfully silly?" Katherine inquired anxiously of Miss Judy later in the afternoon.

"Not a bit," replied Miss Judy emphatically. "He thought that mouse funeral was the best impromptu stunt we've pulled off yet. That kind of thing was just what camp needed today. The novelty of it got everybody stirred up and made them hilarious. That funeral oration of yours was the funniest thing I ever heard. Miss Amesbury thought so too. She took it all down while you were delivering it."

"Daggers and dirks!" exclaimed Katherine, more abashed than ever.

"That made the first coup for the Alley," continued Miss Judy, exulting. "The Avenue is green with envy. They'll rack their brains now to get up something as clever."

"Jane Pratt didn't think it was clever," replied Katherine, trying not to look proud at Miss Judy's compliment. "She said it was the silliest thing she had ever seen."

"Oh, - Jane Pratt!" sniffed Miss Judy, with an expressive shrug of her shoulders. "Jane Pratt would have something sarcastic to say about an archangel. Don't you mind what Jane Pratt says."

From Avernus to Gitchee-Gummee the Alley rang with praises of Katharine's cleverness.

"What's the excitement?" asked Agony wonderingly as she returned to the bungalow in time for supper after resting quietly by herself all day.

"The best thing the Alley ever did!" replied Bengal Virden enthusiastically, and recounted the details for Agony's benefit.

At the same moment someone started a cheer for Katherine down at the other end of the table, and the response was actually deafening:

You're the B-E-S-T, best,
Of all the R-E-S-T, rest,
O, I love you, I love you all the T-I-M-E, time!
If you'll be M-I-N-E, mine,
I'll be T-H-I-N-E, thine,
O, I love you, I love you all the T-I-M-E, time!

Agony cheered with the others, but a little stab of envy went through her breast, a longing to have a cheer thundered at her by the assembled campers, to become prominent, and looked at, and sought after. Sewah had "arrived," and now also Katherine, while she herself was still merely "among those present."

Rather pensively she followed the Winnebagos into Mateka after supper for evening assembly, which had been called by Dr. Grayson. Usually there was no evening assembly; Morning Sing was the only time the whole camp came together in Mateka with the leaders, when all the announcements for the day were made. When there was something special to be announced, however, the bugle sometimes sounded another assembly call at sunset.

"I wonder what the special announcement is tonight?" Hinpoha asked, coming up with Sewah and Agony.

"I don't think it's an announcement at all," replied Sahwah. "I think the professor friend of Dr. Grayson's is going to make a speech. Miss Judy said he always did when he came to camp. He's a naturalist, or something like that."

Agony wrinkled her forehead into a slight frown. "I hope he doesn't," she sighed. "My head still aches and I don't feel like listening to a speech. I'd rather go canoeing up the river, as we had first planned."

She sat down in an inconspicuous corner where she could rest her head upon her drawn up knees, if she wished, without the professor's seeing her, and hoped that the speech would be a short one, and that there would still be time to go canoeing on the river after he had finished.

The professor, however, seemed to have no intention of making a speech. He took a chair beside the fireplace and settled himself in it with the air of one who intended to remain there for some time. It was Dr. Grayson himself who stood up to talk.

"I have called you together," he began, "to tell you about one of the finest actions that has ever been performed by a girl in this camp. I heard about it from the storekeeper at Green's Landing, who was told of it by a man who departed on one of the steamers this morning. This man, who was staying on a farm on the Atlantis Road, and who is suffering from blood-poison in his foot, was taken into the woods in a wheel chair yesterday afternoon and left by himself under a great pine tree at least a hundred feet high. In the topmost branches of this tree a mother robin became tangled up in a string which was caught in a twig, and she hung there by one foot, unable to free herself, fluttering herself to death. At this time two girls came through the path in the woods, took in the situation, and quick as thought one of them climbed the tree, swung herself out on the high branch, and cut the robin loose.

"The man who witnessed the act did not find out the names of the two girls, but the one who climbed the tree wore a Camp Keewaydin hat and a dark green bloomer suit. The other was dressed in brown. I don't think there is anyone who fails to recognize the girl who has done this heroic thing. There is only one green bloomer suit here in camp. Mrs. Grayson tells me that she gave Agnes Wing permission to go to Atlantis with Mary Sylvester yesterday afternoon. Where is she? Agnes Wing, stand up."

Agony stood up in her corner of the room, her lips opened to tell Dr. Grayson that it was Mary who happened to have on the green bloomer suit and had climbed the tree, but her words were drowned in a cheer that nearly raised the roof off the Craft House. Before she knew it Miss Judy and Tiny Armstrong had seized her, set her up on their shoulders, and were carrying her around the room, while the building fairly rocked with applause. Thrilled and intoxicated by the cheering, Agony began to listen to the voice of the tempter in her bosom. No one would ever know that it had not really been she who had done the brave deed; not a soul knew of her lending her suit to Mary because of the mishap in the springhouse. Mary Sylvester was gone; was on her way to Japan; she would never hear about it; and the only person who had witnessed the deed did not know their names; he had only remembered the green bloomer suit. The man himself was unknown, nobody at camp could ever ask him about the affair. He had gone from the neighborhood and would never come face to face with her and discover his mistake; the secret was safe in her heart.

In one bound she could become the most popular girl in camp; gain the favor of the Doctor and the councilors - especially of Miss Amesbury, whom she was most desirous of impressing. The sight of Miss Amesbury leaning forward with shining eyes decided the question for her. The words trembling on her lips were choked back; she hung her head and looked the picture of modest embarrassment, the ideal heroine.

Set down on the floor again by Tiny and Miss Judy, she hid her face on Miss Judy's shoulder and blushed at Dr. Grayson's long speech of praise, in which he spoke touchingly of the beauty of a nature which loved the wild dumb creatures of the woods and sought to protect them from harm; of the cool courage and splendid will power that had sent her out on the shaking branch when her very heart was in her mouth from fear; of the modesty which had kept her silent about the glorious act after she returned to camp. When he took both her hands in his and looked into her face with an expression of admiring regard in his fine, true eyes, she all but told the truth of the matter then and there; but cowardice held her silent and the moment passed.

"Let's have a canoe procession in her honor!" called Miss Judy, and there was a rush for the dock.

Agony was borne down in triumph upon the shoulders of Miss Judy and Tiny, with all the camp marching after, and was set down in the barge of honor, the first canoe behind the towing launch, while all the Alley drew straws for the privilege of riding with her. Still cheering Agony enthusiastically the procession started down the river in a wild, hilarious ride, and Agony thrilled with the joy of being the center of attraction.

"I have arrived at last," she whispered triumphantly to herself as she went to bed that night, and lay awake a long time in the darkness, thinking of the cheers that had rocked the Craft House and of the flattering attention with which Miss Amesbury had regarded her all evening.

Hildegard G. Frey

CHAPTER VII

THE BUSINESS OF BEING A HEROINE

Agony awoke the next morning to find herself famous beyond her fondest dreams. Before she was dressed she saw two of the younger girls peeping into the tent for a glimpse of her; when she stood in line for flag raising she was conscious of eyes turned toward her from all directions while girls who had never noticed her before stopped to say good morning effusively, and seemed inclined to linger in her company; and at breakfast each table in turn sang a cheer for her. Jo Severance, who was one of the acknowledged camp leaders, and whose friendships were not lightly bestowed, ostensibly stopped and waited for Agony to catch up with her on the way over to Morning Sing and walked into Mateka with her arm around Agony's waist.

"Will you be my sleeping partner for the first overnight trip that we take?" she asked cordially.

"Certainly," Agony replied a little breathlessly, already well enough versed in camp customs to realize the extent of the tribute that was being paid her.

At Camp Keewaydin a girl never asked anyone but her dearest friend to be her sleeping partner on an overnight trip, to creep into her poncho sleeping bag with her and share the intimate experience of a night on the ground, heads together on the same pillow, warm bodies touching each other in the crowded nest inside the blankets. And Jo Severance had chosen her to take the place of Mary Sylvester, Jo's own adored Mary, who was to have been Jo's partner on all occasions!

Before Morning Sing was over Agony had received a dozen pressing invitations to share beds on that first camping trip, and the date of the trip was not even announced yet!

And to all this fuss and favor Agony responded like a prism placed in the sunlight. She sparkled, she glowed, she radiated, she brought to the surface with a rush all the wit and charm and talent that lay in her being. She beamed upon everyone right and left; she threw herself with ardor and enthusiasm into every plan that was suggested; she had a dozen brilliant ideas in as many minutes; she seemed absolutely inspired. Her deep voice came out so strongly that she was able to carry the alto in the singing against the whole camp; she improvised delightful harmonies that put a thrill into the commonest tune. She got up of her own accord and performed the gestures to "The Lone Fish Ball" better even than Mary Sylvester had done them, and on the spur of the moment she worked out another set to accompany "The Bulldog and the Bullfrog" that brought down the house. It took only the stimulating influence of the limelight to bring out and intensify every talent she had ever possessed. It worked upon her like a drug, quickening her faculties, spurring her on to one brilliant performance after the other, while the camp looked upon her in wonder as one gifted by the gods.

The same exalted mood possessed her during swimming hour, and she passed the test for Sharks with flying colors. Immediately afterward she completed the canoe test and joined that envied class who were allowed to take out a canoe on their own responsibility.

A dozen new admirers flocked around her as she walked back to Gitchee-Gummee at the close of the Swimming hour, all begging to be allowed to sew up the tear in her bathing suit, or offering to lend her the prettiest of their bathing caps. What

Hildegard G. Frey

touched Agony most, however, was the pride which the Winnebagos took in her exploit.

"We knew you would do something splendid sometime and bring honor to us," they told her exultingly, with shining faces.

"I'm going to write Nyoda about it this minute," said Migwan, after she had finished her words of praise. "What's the mater, Agony, have you a headache again?" she finished.

"No," replied Agony in a tone of forced carelessness.

"I thought maybe you had," continued Migwan solicitously. "Your forehead was all puckered up."

"The light is so bright on the river," murmured Agony, and walked thoughtfully away.

Days passed in pleasant succession; Mary Sylvester's name gradually ceased to be heard on all sides from her mourning cronies, who at first accompanied every camp activity with a plaintive chorus of, "Remember the way Mary used to do this," or "Oh, I wish Mary were here to enjoy this," or "Mary had planned to do this the first chance she got," and so on. Life in camp was so packed full of enjoyment for those who remained behind that it was impossible to go on missing the departed one indefinitely.

The first camping trip was a thing of the past. It had been a twenty-mile hike along the river to a curious group of rocks known as "Hercules' Library," from the resemblance which the granite blocks bore to shelves of books. Here, among these fantastic formations, the camp had spread its blankets and literally snored, if not actually upon, at least at the base of, the flint.

When bedtime came Katherine had found herself without a sleeping partner, for she had forgotten to ask someone herself, and it just happened that no one had asked her. She was philosophically trying to make her bed up for a single, by doubling the poncho over lengthwise into a cocoon effect, when she heard a sniffle coming out of the bushes beside her. Investigating, she found Carmen Chadwick sitting disconsolately upon a very much wrinkled poncho, her chin in her hands, the picture of woe.

"What's the matter, can't you make your bed?" asked Katherine, remembering Carmen's helplessness in that line upon a former occasion.

"I haven't any partner!" answered Carmen, with another sniffle. "I had one, but she's run away from me."

"Who was it?" asked Katherine.

"Jane Pratt," replied Carmen. "I asked her a long time ago if I might sleep with her on the first trip, and she said, certainly I might, and she would bring along enough blankets for the two of us, and I wouldn't need to bother bringing any. So I didn't bring any blankets; but when I asked her just now where we were going to sleep, she said she hadn't the faintest notion where *I* was going to sleep, but *she* was going to sleep alone in the woods, away from the rest of us. She laughed at me, and said she never intended to bring along enough blankets for the two of us, and that I should have known better than to believe her. What shall I do?" she wailed, beginning to weep in earnest.

Katherine gave vent to an exclamation that sent a nearby chipmunk scampering away in a panic. She looked around for Miss Judy, but Miss Judy was deep in the woods with the other councilors getting up a stunt to entertain the girls after supper. "Where's Jane Pratt?" asked Katherine.

"I don't know," sniffled Carmen.

"Didn't you bring any blankets at all?"

"No."

"Carmen, didn't it ever occur to you that Jane was making fun of you when she said she would bring blankets for two? Nobody ever does that, you know, they'd make too heavy a load to carry."

Carmen shook her head, and gulped afresh.

"No, I never thought of that. I wanted a sleeping partner so badly, and everyone I asked was already engaged, and when she said yes I was *so* happy."

"Of all the mean, contemptible tricks to play on a poor little creature like that!" Katherine exclaimed aloud.

"What's the matter?" asked Agony, appearing beside her.

Katherine told her.

Agony's eyes flashed. "I'm going to find Jane Pratt," she said in the calm tone which always indicated smouldering anger, "and make her share her blankets with Carmen."

Jane, who, with the practised eye of the old camper, had selected a smooth bit of ground thickly covered with pine needles and sloping gently upward toward the end for her head, and had arranged her two double blankets and her extra large sized poncho into an extremely comfortable bed for one, looked up from her labors to find Agony standing before her with flushed face and blazing eyes.

"Jane Pratt," Agony began without preliminary, "did you promise to sleep with Carmen Chadwick, and lead her to think she did not need to bring any blankets along on this trip?"

Jane returned Agony's gaze coolly, and gave a slight, disagreeable laugh. "Carmen's the biggest goose in camp," she said scornfully. "Anybody'd know I didn't mean -"

"*Carmen* didn't know you didn't mean it," Agony interrupted. "She thought you were sincere, and believed you, and now she's dreadfully hurt about it. You ought to be ashamed of yourself, hurting a poor little girl's feelings like that."

"If anybody's green enough to come on an overnight trip without any blankets and actually think someone else is going to bring them for her -"

"Well, as it happens, Carmen *was* green enough, and that's just the point. She's never been away from home and because she's so desperately homesick she's having a hard time making friends. If one person treats her like this it'll be hard for her ever to believe what people tell her and it'll be harder for her to get acquainted than ever."

Jane shrugged her shoulders. "What she believes or doesn't believe doesn't concern me."

"Why, Jane Pratt!"

Jane smiled amusedly at Agony's reproachful exclamation. "My dear," she said patronizingly, "I never sleep with anyone. There's no one I like well enough. I thought everyone in camp knew that."

"Then why did you tell Carmen you would sleep with her?"

"Because she's such a goose it was no end of fun taking her in."

"Then you deliberately deceived her?" asked Agony witheringly.

"Well, and what if I did?" retorted Jane.

"You have absolutely no sense of honor," Agony remarked contemptuously. "Deceiving people is just as bad as lying, or cheating."

Stung by Agony's tone, Jane flushed a little. "Well, what do you expect me to do about it?" she demanded. "What business is it of yours, anyway?"

"You're going to let Carmen take one of your blankets,' replied Agony.

"I'll do no such thing," returned Jane flatly. "It's going to be cold here tonight and I'll need them both."

"And what about Carmen?"

"Bother Carmen! If she's such a goose to think that I meant what I said she deserves to be cold."

"Why, Jane Pratt!"

"Why don't you share your own blankets with her, if you're so concerned about her?"

"I'm perfectly willing to, and so are the rest of the girls, but we're giving you the *opportunity* to do it, to help right the mistake."

"I suppose you've told all the girls in camp about it and will run and tell Mrs. Grayson to come and make me give up my blankets."

"I'll do no such thing. If you aren't kind hearted enough yourself to want to make Carmen feel better it wouldn't mend matters any to have Mrs. Grayson make you do it. But I shall certainly let the girls know about it. I think they ought to know what an amiable disposition you have. I don't think you'll be bothered with any more overtures of friendship."

Jane yawned. "For goodness' sake, are you going to preach all night? That voice of yours sets my nerves on edge. Take a blanket and present it to Carmen with my love - and let me alone." She stripped the top blanket from her bed and threw it at Agony's feet; then walked off, calling over her shoulder as she went, "Good bye, Miss Champion of simple camp infants. Most courageous, most honorable!"

She did not see the sudden spasm that contorted Agony's face at the word "honorable." It suddenly came over Agony that she had no right to be calling other people cheats and liars and taking them to task about their sense of honor, she, who was enjoying honors that did not belong to her. The light of victory faded from her eyes; the angry flush died away on her cheek. Very quietly she stole back to Carmen and held the blanket out to her.

"Jane's sorry she can't sleep with you, because she never sleeps well and is apt to disturb people, but she's willing to let you take one of her blankets," she said gently.

"Oh, thank you!" said Carmen, much comforted. "I'm going to sleep with Katherine. With this blanket there'll be enough bedding to make a double. I'm glad I'm not going to sleep with Jane," she confided to Katherine. "I'm afraid of her. I would lots rather have had you for my partner from the beginning, but I was afraid to ask you because I was sure you were promised to somebody else."

"Motto," said Katherine, laughing. "Faint heart never won lanky lady. Don't ever hesitate to ask me anything again. Come on, let's get this bed made up in a hurry. I see the councilors coming back. That means their show is going to commence."

Of course, it was not long before Agony's little passage of arms with Jane Pratt in behalf of timid little Carmen was known all over camp, and Agony went up another point in popular favor as Jane Pratt went down. The councilors heard about it, too, for whatever Bengal Virden knew was promptly confided to Pom-pom. Miss Judy told it to Dr. Grayson, and he nodded his head approvingly.

"It's no more than you would expect from the girl who rescued that robin," he said warmly. "The champion of all weaker creatures. Diplomatic, too. Tried to save Carmen's feelings in the matter by not telling her the exact spirit in which Jane gave up the blanket. A good leader; another Mary Sylvester."

Then, turning to Mrs. Grayson, he asked plaintively: "Mother, *why* do we have to be afflicted with Jane Pratt year after year? She's been a thorn in our flesh for the past three summers."

"I have told you before," replied Mrs. Grayson resignedly, "that I only accept her because she is the daughter of my old friend Anne Dudley. I cannot offend Mrs. Pratt because I am under various obligations to her, so for the sake of her mother we must continue to be afflicted with Jane Pratt."

Dr. Grayson heaved a long sigh, and muttered something about "the fell clutch of circumstance."

"We seem rather plentifully saddled with 'obligations,'" he remarked a moment later.

"Meaning?" inquired Mrs. Grayson.

"Claudia Peckham," rejoined the Doctor. "Sweet Claudia Peckham: How she used to scrap with my little brothers when she came to visit us! She had a disposition like the bubonic plague when she was little, and by all the signs she doesn't seem to have mellowed any with age."

"Doctor!" exclaimed Mrs. Grayson reprovingly.

"Sad, but true," continued the Doctor, his eyes twinkling reminiscently. "When she came to visit us the cat used to hide her kittens under the porch, and the whole household went into a regular state of siege. By the way, how is she getting on? I've lived in fear of the explosion every minute. I never thought she'd last this long. Who has she in the tent with her?"

"That brown haired madonna you think is so sweet, and the pretty, golden haired girl who is her intimate friend," replied Mrs. Grayson. "Those two, and - Bengal Virden."

The Doctor gave vent to a long whistle. "Bengal Virden in the same tent with Claudia Peckham? And the tent is still standing?"

"Bengal doesn't sleep in the tent," admitted Mrs. Grayson. "She has moved underneath it, into a couch hammock. She thinks I don't know it, but under the circumstances I shall not interfere. We have to keep Cousin Claudia *somewhere*, and as long as they'll put up with her in Ponemah I don't care how they manage it. She *would* be a tent councilor."

"How do the other two get along with her?" asked the Doctor, "the two that have not moved underneath, as yet?"

"I don't know," replied Mrs. Grayson in a frankly puzzled tone. "They must be angels unaware, that's all I can say."

CHAPTER VIII

THE SHOE BEGINS TO PINCH

"Tramp, tramp, tramp, the bugs are marching,
Up and down the tents they go,
Some are brown and some are black,
But of each there is no lack,
And the Daddy-long-legs they go marching too!"

So sang Sahwah as she tidied up her tent after Morning Sing. It was war on bugs and spiders this morning; war to the knife, or rather, to the broom. Usually there was no time between Morning Sing and tent inspection to do more than give the place a swift tidying up; to sweep the floor and straighten up the beds and set the table in order. Bugs and spiders did not count against one in tent inspection, being looked upon as circumstances over which one had no control; hence no one ever bothered about them. But that morning Sahwah, lying awake waiting for the rising bugle to blow, saw a round-bellied, jolly-looking little bug crawling leisurely along the floor, dragging a tiny seed of grain with him, and looking for all the world like the father of a family bringing a loaf of bread home for breakfast. As she watched it traveling along a crack in the board floor, a very large, fierce-looking bug appeared on the scene, fell upon the smaller one, killed and half devoured it, and then made off triumphantly with the seed the other had been carrying.

"No you don't!" shouted Sahwah aloud, waking Agony out of

a sound sleep.

"What's the matter?" yawned Agony.

Sahwah laughed a little foolishly. "It was nothing; only a bug," she explained. "I'm sorry I wakened you, Agony. You see, I was watching a cute little bug carrying a seed across the floor, and a bigger bug came along and took it away from him. I won't stand for anything like that here in Gitchee-Gummee. We all play fair here, and nobody takes any plums that belong to someone else."

She rose in her wrath, reached for her shoe, and made short work of the unethical despoiler.

Agony made no comment. The words, *we all play fair here, and nobody takes any plums that belong to someone else,* pierced her bosom like barbed arrows. She lay so still that Sahwah thought she had dropped off to sleep again, and crept quietly back to bed so as not to disturb her a second time. Like the tiger, however, who, once having tasted blood, is consumed with the lust of killing, Sahwah, having squashed one bug, itched to do the same with all the others in the tent, and when tidying-up time came there began a ruthless campaign of extermination.

Agony, having made her bed and swept out underneath it, departed abruptly from the scene. Somehow the sight of bugs being killed was upsetting to her just now. She wandered down toward the river, listening pensively to the sweet piping notes of Noel Sanderson's whistle, coming from somewhere along the shore; then she turned and walked toward Mateka, planning to put in some time working on the design for her paddle before Craft Hour began and the place became filled to overflowing with other designers, all wanting the design books and the rulers and compasses at once.

As she passed under the balcony which was Miss Amesbury's sanctum, a cordial hail floated down from above. "Good morning, Agony, whither bound so early, and what means that portentous frown?"

Agony looked up to see Miss Amesbury, wreathed in smiles, peering down over the rustic railing at her. Agony flushed with pleasure at the cordiality of the tone, and the use of her nickname. It was only the girls for which she had a special liking that Miss Amesbury ever addressed by a nickname, no matter how universally in use that nickname might be with the rest of the camp. Agony's blood tingled with a sense of triumph; her eyes sparkled and her face took on that look of being lighted up from within that characterized her in moments of great animation.

"I was coming down to Mateka to put in some extra work on the design for my paddle," she replied, in her rich, vibrating voice, "and I was frowning because I was a little puzzled how I was going to work it out."

"Industrious child!" replied Miss Amesbury. "Come up and visit me and I'll show you some good designs for paddles."

The next half hour was so filled with delight for Agony that she did not know whether she was sleeping or waking. Sitting opposite her adored Miss Amesbury on a rustic bench covered with a bright Indian blanket and listening to the fascinating conversation of this much traveled, older woman, the voice of conscience grew fainter and nearly ceased tormenting Agony altogether, and she gave herself up wholly to the enjoyment of the moment. In answer to Miss Amesbury's questioning, she told of her home and school life; her great admiration for Edwin Langham; and about the Winnebagos and their good times; and Miss Amesbury laughed heartily at her tales and in turn related her own school-girl pranks and enthusiasm in a flattering confidential way.

Agony rushed up to the Winnebagos after Craft Hour, radiant with pride and happiness. "Miss Amesbury invited me up to her balcony," she announced, trying hard to speak casually, "and she lent me one of her own books to read, and she helped me work out the design for my paddle. She's the most wonderful woman I've ever met. She wants me to come again often, she says, and she invited me to go walking with her in the woods this afternoon to get some balsam."

"O Agony, how splendid!" cried Migwan, with a hint of wistfulness in her voice. Migwan did not envy Agony her sudden popularity with the campers one bit; that was her just due after the splendid deed she had performed; but where Miss Amesbury was concerned Migwan could not help feeling a few pangs of jealousy. She admired Miss Amesbury with all the passion that was in her, looking up to her as one of the nameless, insignificant stars of heaven might look up to the Evening Star; she prayed that Miss Amesbury might single her out for intimate friendship such as was enjoyed by Mary Sylvester and some of the other older girls. Migwan never breathed this desire to anyone, but if Miss Amesbury had only known it, a certain pair of soft brown eyes rested eagerly upon her all through Morning Sing, as she sat at the piano playing hymns and choruses, even as they were fixed upon her during meals and other assemblies. And now the thing that Migwan coveted so much had come to Agony, and Agony basked in the light of Miss Amesbury's twinkling smile and enjoyed all the privileges of friendship which Migwan would have given her right hand to possess. But, being Migwan, she bravely brushed aside her momentary feeling of envy, told herself sternly that if she was worth it Miss Amesbury would notice her sooner or later, and cheerfully lent Agony her best pencil to transfer the new paddle design with.

"Supper on the water tonight!" announced Miss Judy, going the rounds late in the afternoon. "Everybody go down on the dock when the supper bugle blows, instead of coming into the dining room."

There was a mad rush for canoe partners, and a hasty gathering together of guitars and mandolins, which would certainly be in demand for the evening sing-out which would follow supper. Agony, being in an exalted mood, had an inspiration, which she confided to Gladys in a whisper, and Gladys, nodding, moved off in the direction of the Bungalow and paid a visit to her trunk up in the loft, after which she and Agony disappeared into the woods.

The river was bathed in living fire from the rays of the setting sun when the little fleet of boats pushed out from the shore and began circling around the floating dock where Miss Judy and Tiny Armstrong, with the help of three or four other councilors, were passing out plates of salad, sandwiches and cups of milk. Having received their supplies, the canoes backed away and went moving up or down the river as the paddlers desired, sometimes two or three canoes close together, sometimes one alone, but all, whether alone or in groups, filling the occupants of the launch with desperate envy. A dozen or more girls these were, still in the Minnow class, still denied the privilege of going out in a canoe because they had not yet passed the swimming test.

Oh-Pshaw, alas, was still one of them. She looked wistfully at Agony, a Shark, in charge of a canoe with Hinpoha and Gladys and Jo Severance as companions, gliding alongside of Sahwah and Undine Cirelle on the one side and Katherine and Jean Lawrence on the other. She heard their voices floating across the water as they laughingly called to each other and sang snatches of songs aimed at Miss Judy and Tiny Armstrong on the floating dock; heard Tiny Armstrong remark to Miss Judy, "There's the best group of canoeists we've ever had in camp. Won't they make a showing on Regatta Day, though!"

Oh-Pshaw longed with all her heart on floating supper nights to belong to that illustrious company and go gliding up and down the river like a swan instead of chugging around in the launch, sitting cramped up to make room for the supper supplies that covered the floor on the trip out, and baskets of used forks and spoons and cups on the trip back. It was not a brilliant company that went in the launch. Jacob, Dr. Grayson's helper about camp, ran the engine. Being desperately shy, he attended strictly to business, and never so much as glanced at the girls packed in behind him. Half a dozen of the younger camp girls, who never did anything but whisper together, carve stones for their favorite councilors, and giggle continually; three or four of the older girls who sat silent as clams for the most part, and never betrayed any particular enthusiasm, no matter what went on; Carmen Chadwick, who clung to Oh-Pshaw and squeaked with alarm every time the launch changed her course; and Miss Peckham, who from her seat in the stern kept shouting nervous admonitions at the unheeding Jacob; these constituted the company who were doomed to travel together on all excursions.

Oh-Pshaw labored heroically to infuse a spark of life into the company; she wrote a really clever little song about "the Exclusive Crew of the Irish Stew," but she could not induce the exclusive crew to sing it, so her first poetic effort was love's labor lost. So she looked enviously upon the canoes and resolved more firmly than ever to overcome her fear of the water and learn to swim, and thus have done with the launch and its uninspiring company for all time.

Migwan's eyes, as usual, went roving in search of Miss Amesbury, but tonight, to her sorrow, they did not find her anywhere in the canoes.

"Where is Miss Amesbury?" she asked of Miss Judy, as her canoe came up alongside of the "lunch counter."

"She didn't come out with us tonight," replied Miss Judy, tipping the milk can far over to pour out the last drop. "She wanted to do some writing, she said."

Migwan sighed quietly and gave herself over to being agreeable to her canoe mates, but the occasion had lost its savor for her.

Supper finished, the canoes began to drift westward toward the setting sun, following the broad streak of light that lay like a magic highway upon the water, while guitars and mandolins began to tinkle, and from all around clear girlish voices, blended together in exquisite harmony, took up song after song.

"Oh, I could float along like this and sing forever!" breathed Hinpoha, picking out soft chords on her guitar, and looking dreamily at the evening star glowing like a jewelled lamp in the western sky.

"So could I," replied Migwan, leaning back in the canoe with her hands clasped behind her head, and letting the light breeze ruffle the soft tendrils of hair around her temples. "It is going to be full moon tonight," she added. "See, there it is, rising above the treetops. How big and bright it is! Can it be possible that it is only a mass of dead chalk and not a ball of burnished silver? Gladys will enjoy that moon, she always loves it so when it is so big and round and bright. By the way, where *is* Gladys? I saw her in a canoe not long ago, but I don't see her anywhere now."

"I don't know where she is," replied Hinpoha, glancing idly around at the various craft and then letting her eyes rest upon the moon again.

The little fleet had rounded an island and turned back upstream, now traveling in the silver moon-path, now gliding through velvety black shadows, and was approaching a long, low ledge of rock that jutted out into the water just beyond the big bend in the river. A sudden exclamation of "Ah-h!" drew everybody's attention to the rock, and there a wondrous spectacle presented itself - a white robed figure dancing in the moonlight as lighty as a bit of seafoam, her filmy draperies fluttering in the wind, her long yellow hair twined with lillies.

"Who is it?" several voices cried in wonder, and the paddlers stopped spellbound with their paddles poised in air.

"Gladys!" exclaimed Migwan. "I thought she was planning a surprise, she and Agony were whispering together this afternoon. Isn't she wonderful, though!" Migwan's voice rang with pride in her beloved friend's accomplishment. "Too bad Miss Amesbury isn't here to see it."

The dancer on the rock dipped and swayed and whirled in a mad measure, finally disappearing into the shadow of a towering cliff, from whence she emerged a few moments later, once more in the canoe with Agony, and changed back from a water nymph into a Camp Keewaydin girl in middy and bloomers.

"It was Agony's idea," she explained simply, in response to the storm of applause that greeted her reappearance among the girls. "She thought of it this afternoon when the word went around that we were going to have supper on the water."

Then Agony came in for her share of the applause also, until the woods echoed to the sound of cheering.

"Too bad Miss Amesbury had to miss it." Thus Agony echoed Migwan's earlier expression of regret as she walked down the Alley arm in arm with Migwan and Hinpoha after the first bugle. "She's been working up there on her balcony all evening, and didn't hear a bit of the singing. We were too far up the river."

"Couldn't we sing a bit for her?" suggested Migwan. "Serenade her, I mean; just a few of us who are used to singing together?"

"Good idea," replied Agony enthusiastically. "Get all the Winnebagos together and let's sing her some of our own songs, the ones we've practicsed so much together at home. You bring your mandolin, Migs, and tell Hinpoha to bring her guitar. Hurry, we'll have to do it fast to get back for lights out."

Miss Amesbury, wearily finishing her evening's work, was suddenly greeted by a burst of song from beneath her balcony; a surpassing deep, rich alto, beautifully blended with a number of clear, pure sopranos, accompanied by mandolin and guitar. It was a song she had not heard in years, one which held a beautiful, tender association for her:

> "I would that my love could silently
> Flow in a single word -"

A mist came over her eyes as she listened, and the gates of memory swung back on their golden hinges, revealing another scene, when she had listened to that song sung by a voice now long since hushed. She put her hand over her eyes as if in pain, then dropped it slowly into her lap and sat leaning back in her chair listening with hungry ears to the familiar strains. When the last note had echoed itself quite away she leaned over the balcony and called down softly, "Thanks, many thanks, girls. You do not know what a treat you have given me. Who are you? I know one of you must be Agony, I recognize her alto, but who are the rest of you? The Winnebagos? I might have guessed it. You are dear girls to think of me up here by myself and to put yourselves out to give me pleasure. Come and visit me in the daytime, every one of you. There goes the last bugle. Goodnight, girls. Thank you a thousand times!"

The Winnebagos scurried off toward the Alley, in high spirits at the success of their little plan. Migwan actually trembled with joy. At last she had been invited up on Miss Amesbury's fascinating little balcony. True, the invitation had been a general one to all the Winnebagos, but nevertheless, it was a beginning.

"Miss Amesbury must have been very tired tonight," she confided to Hinpoha. "Her voice actually shook when she thanked us for singing."

"I noticed it, too," replied Hinpoha, beginning to pull her middy off over her head as she walked along.

When Agony reached the door of Gitchee-Gummee she remembered that she had left her camp hat lying in the path below Mateka, where they had stood to serenade Miss Amesbury, and fearing that the wind, which was increasing in velocity, might blow it into the river before morning, she hastened back to rescue it. She moved quietly, for it was after lights out and she did not wish to disturb the camp. Miss Amesbury's lamp was extinguished and her balcony was shrouded in darkness by the shadow of the tall pine which grew against it.

"She must be very tired," thought Agony, remembering Migwan's words, "and is already in bed."

Agony felt carefully over the shadowy ground for her hat, found it and started back up the path. But the beauty of the moonlight on the river tempted her to loiter and dream along the bluff before returning to her tent. Enchanted by the magic scene beneath her, she stood still and gazed for many minutes at the gleaming river of water which seemed to her like pure molten silver.

As she stood gazing, half lost in dreams, she saw a canoe shoot out from the opposite shore some distance up the river and come toward Keewaydin, keeping in the shadows along the shore. Just before it reached camp it drew in and discharged a passenger, which Agony could see was a girl. Then the canoe put off again, and as it crossed a moonlit place Agony saw that it was painted bright red, the color of the canoes belonging to the Boy's Camp located about a half mile down the river. Agony realized what the presence of that canoe meant. One of the girls of Keewaydin had been out canoeing on the sly with some boy from Camp Alamont - a thing forbidden in the Keewaydin code - and was being brought back in this surreptitious manner. Who could the girl be? Agony grimaced with disgust. She waited quietly there in the path where the girl, whoever she was, must pass in order to go up to her tent. In a few moments the girl came along and nearly stumbled over her in the darkness, crying out in alarm at the unexpected encounter. Agony's swiftly adjusted flashlight fell upon the heavy features and unpleasant eyes of Jane Pratt.

"O Jane," cried Agony, " you haven't been over at that boys' camp, have you? You surely know it's forbidden - Dr. Grayson said so distinctly when he read the camp rules."

"Well, what if I have?" Jane demanded in a tone of asperity. "Dr. Grayson makes a lot of rules that are too silly for words. I have a friend over at Camp Altamont that I've known for years and if I choose to go canoeing with him on such a gorgeous night instead of going to bed at nine o'clock like a baby it's nobody's business. By the way, what are *you* doing here?" she demanded suspiciously. "Why aren't you in bed with the rest of the infants?"

"I came out to get my hat," replied Agony simply.

"Strange thing that your hat should get lost just in the spot where I happen to come ashore," remarked Jane sarcastically. "How long have you been spying upon my movements, Miss Virtue?"

"I haven't been spying on you," declared Agony hotly. "I hadn't any idea you were out. To tell the truth, I never missed you this evening when we were on the river."

"Well, I suppose you'll pull Mrs. Grayson out of her bed now to tell her the scandal about Jane Pratt," continued Jane bitingly, "and tomorrow morning at five o'clock there'll be another departure from camp."

"O Jane!" cried Agony, in distress. "Will she really send you home?"

"She really will," mocked Jane. "She sent a girl home last year who did the same thing."

"O Jane, how dreadful that would be," said Agony.

"And how sorry you would be to have me go - not," returned Jane derisively.

"Jane," said Agony seriously, "if I promise not to tell Mrs. Grayson this time will you promise never to do this sort of thing again? It would be awful to be sent home from camp in disgrace. If you think it over you'll surely see what a much better time you'll have if you don't break rules - if you work and play honorably. Won't you please try?"

The derisive tone deepened in Jane's voice as she answered, "No I will *not*. I'll make no such babyish promise - to you of all people - because I wouldn't keep it if I did make it."

"Then," said Agony firmly, "I'll do just as we do in school with the honor system. I'll give you three days to tell Mrs. Grayson yourself, and if you haven't done it by the end of that time I'll tell her myself. What you are doing is a bad example for the younger girls, and Mrs. Grayson ought to know about it."

Jane's only reply was a mocking laugh as she brushed past Agony and went in the direction of her tent.

CHAPTER IX

AN EXPLORING TRIP

"Miss Amesbury wants us to go off on a canoe trip with her," announced Agony, rushing up to the Winnebagos after Craft Hour the next morning.

"Wants who to go on a canoe trip with her?" demanded Sahwah in excitement.

"Why, us, the Winnebagos," replied Agony. "Just us, and Jo Severance. She wants to take a canoe trip up the river, but she doesn't want to go with the whole camp when they go because there will be too much noise and excitement. She wants a quieter trip, but she doesn't want to go all alone, so she has asked Dr. Grayson if she may take us girls. He said she might. We're to start this afternoon, right after dinner, and be gone over night; maybe two nights."

"O Agony!" breathed Migwan in ecstacy, falling upon Agony's neck and hugging her rapturously. "It's all due to you. If you hadn't done that splendid thing we wouldn't be half as popular as we are. We're sharing your glory with you." She smiled fondly into Agony's eyes and squeezed her hand heartily. "Good old Agony," she murmured.

Agony smiled back mechanically and returned the squeeze with only a slight pressure. "Nonsense," she replied with emphasis. "It isn't on account of what - I - did at all that she has asked you. It's because you serenaded her the other evening. That was *your* doing, Migwan."

"But we wouldn't have ventured to serenade her if she hadn't been so friendly with you," replied Migwan, "so it amounts to the same thing in the end. That's the way it has always been with us Winnebagos, hasn't it? What one does always helps the rest of us. Sahwah's swimming has made us all famous; and so has Gladys's dancing and Katherine's speechifying."

"And your writing," put in Hinpoha. "Don't forget that Indian legend of yours that brought the spotlight down upon us in our freshman year. That was really the making of us. No matter what one of us does, the others all share in the glory."

A tiny shiver went down Agony's back. "And I suppose," she added casually, "if one of us were to disgrace herself the others would share the disgrace."

"We certainly would," said Sahwah with conviction.

Agony turned away with a dry feeling in her throat and walked soberly to her tent to prepare for the canoe trip.

"Have you noticed that there is something queer about Agony lately?" Migwan remarked to Gladys as she laid out her poncho on the tent floor preparatory to rolling it.

"I haven't noticed it," replied Gladys, getting out needle and thread to sew up a small rent in her bloomers. "What do you mean?"

"Why, I can't explain it exactly," continued Migwan, pausing in the act of doubling back her blanket to fit the shape of the poncho, "but she's different, somehow. She sits and stares out over the river sometimes for half an hour at a stretch, and sometimes when you speak to her she gives you an answer that shows she hasn't heard what you said."

"I *have* noticed it, now that you speak of it," replied Gladys, straightening up from her mending job to give Migwan a hand with the poncho rolling. Then she added, "Maybe she's in love. Those are supposed to be the symptoms, aren't they?"

"Gracious!" exclaimed Migwan in a startled tone. "Do you suppose that can be what's the matter with her. I hadn't thought of that."

"It must be," said Gladys with a quaint air of wordly wisdom, and then the two girls proceeded to forget Agony in the labor of rolling the poncho up neatly and making it fast with a piece of rope tied in a square knot.

When Agony reached Gitchee-Gummee on her errand of packing, there was Jo Severance waiting for her with a letter.

"Letter from Mary Sylvester," she called gaily, waving it over her head. "It just came in the morning's mail and I haven't opened it yet. Thought I'd bring it down and let you read it with me."

An icy hand seemed to clutch at Agony's heart, and she gazed at the little white linen paper envelope as though it might contain a bomb. Here was a danger she had not foreseen. Mary Sylvester, even though she had left camp, corresponded with her bosom friend, Jo Severance, and very naturally she might make some reference to the robin incident. Agony gazed in fascinated silence as Jo opened the envelope with a nail file in lieu of a paper cutter and spread out the pages. Little black specks began to float before her eyes and she leaned against the bed to steady herself for the blow which she felt in her prophetic soul was coming. Jo, in her eagerness to read the letter, noticed nothing out of the way in Agony's expression. Dropping down on the bed beside her she began to read aloud:

"Dearest Jo:

"When I think of you and all the other dear people I

left behind me in camp it seems that I must fly right
back to Keewaydin. It still seems a dream, my coming
away so soon after arriving. I have done nothing but
rush around since, getting my things together. We are in
San Francisco now, and sail tonight." ...

So the letter ran for several pages - descriptions of things she
had seen on the trip west, and loving messages for her friends
at Camp, and closing with a hasty "Goodbye, Jo dear." Not a
word about the robin. The choking sensation in Agony's
throat left her. Weak-kneed, she sank down on the bed and lay
back on the pillow, closing her eyes wearily. Unnoticing, Jo
departed to show the letter to the girls to whom Mary had sent
messages.

Agony lay very still, thinking. Even if Mary had not mentioned
the robin incident in this letter, she might in a later one; the
danger was never really over. And on the other hand, Jo
Severance, dear Jo, who had become so fond of Agony in the
last few weeks, would certainly tell Mary about the robin when
she answered her letter. Jo had already written it to her mother
and to several friends, she had told her. Jo never grew tired of
talking about it, and displayed a touching pride in having
Agony for an intimate friend. Yes, without doubt Jo would
write it to Mary, and then Mary would write back and tell the
truth. Agony grew hot and cold by turns as she lay there
thinking of the certainty of exposure. What a blind fool she
had been. If only she had told the story the minute she got
home that day, instead of keeping it to herself, then the
moment of temptation would never have come to her. If only
Mary hadn't been called away just then!

Could she still take the story back, she wondered, and tell it as
it really had been? Her heart sank at the thought and her pride
cried out against it. No, she could never stand the disgrace.
But what if the truth were to leak out through Mary - that
would be infinitely worse. Her thoughts went around in a
torturing circle and brought her to no decision. Should she
make a clean breast of it now and have nothing more to fear,

Hildegard G. Frey

or should she take a chance on Jo's never mentioning it to Mary?

While she was debating the question back and forth in her mind Bengal Virden came running into the tent. Bengal was beginning to tag after Agony as she had formerly tagged after Mary Sylvester. Agony often caught the younger girl's eyes fastened upon her with an expression of worship that fairly embarrassed her. It was the first real crush that a younger girl had ever had on Agony, and although Agony laughed about it to her friends, she still derived no small amount of satisfaction from it, and had resolved to be a real influence for good to stout, fly-away Bengal.

The girl came running in now with a leaf cup full of red, ripe raspberries in her hand, and laid it in Agony's lap. "I picked them all for you," she remarked, looking at Agony with an adoring gaze.

"Oh, thank you," said Agony, sitting up and fingering the tempting gift. She selected a large ripe berry and put it into her mouth, giving an involuntary exclamation of pleasure at the fine, rich flavor of the fruit. This, she reflected, was the reward of popularity - the cream of all good things from the hands of her admirers. Could she give it up - could she bear to see their admiration turn to scorn?

"And Agony," begged Bengal, "may I have a lock of your hair to keep?" The depths of adoration expressed in that request sent an odd thrill through Agony. She knew then that she could not bear it to have Bengal be disappointed in her; could not let her know that she was only posing as a heroine. The die was cast. She would take her chance on no one's ever finding it out.

Right after dinner the little voyaging party pushed out from the dock and headed upstream; three canoes side by side with ponchos and provisions stowed away under the seats, and the Winnebago banner trailing from the stern of the "flagship,' the one in which Miss Amesbury rode, with Sahwah and Migwan as paddlers. Migwan and Hinpoha had constructed the banner in record time that morning, giving up their swimming hour to finish it. No Winnebago expedition should ever start out without a banner flying; they would just as soon have gone without their shoes. Oh-Pshaw waved them a brave farewell from the dock, philosophically accepting the fact that she could not go in a canoe and making no fuss about it.

Jo Severance, who had paddled up the river before, and knew its course thoroughly, acted as guide and pilot. For the first night's camping ground they were going to a place where Jo had camped on a former trip, a place which she enthusiastically described as "just made for four beds to be spread in." It had all the conveniences of home, she assured them; a nearby spring for drinking water and a good place to swim, and what more could anyone want!

By common consent they paddled slowly at the outset, wisely refraining from exhausting their strength in the first mile or so, as is so apt to be the case with inexperienced paddlers. The Winnebagos had paddled together so often that it was unnecessary for them to count aloud to keep together; the six paddles flashed and dipped as one in time to some mysterious inner rhythm, sending the three canoes forward with a smooth, even motion, and keeping their noses almost in a straight line across the river.

"How beautifully you pull together!" exclaimed Miss Amesbury in admiration, leaning back and watching the six brown arms rising and falling in unison.

"We're used to pulling together," said Sahwah simply.

The boys from Camp Altamont were at their swimming hour when they passed, and hailed them with great shouting, which they returned with a camp cheer and a salute with the paddles. The red canoes were drawn up in a line on the dock and Agony wondered which one it was that had made the stealthy voyage to Camp Keewaydin the night before. This brought back to her mind the subject of Jane Pratt, and she wondered if Jane had really taken her seriously when she had demanded that she confess her breaking of the camp rule; if Jane would really tell Mrs. Grayson herself, or force her to inform upon her. It came over her rather forcefully that she was not exactly in a position to be telling tales about other deceivers - that she was in their class herself.

"Why so pensive?" inquired Miss Amesbury brightly, as Agony paddled along in silence, looking straight ahead of her and paying no attention to the gay conversation going on all about her.

Agony collected herself and smiled brightly at Miss Amesbury. "I was just thinking," she replied composedly. "Did I look glum? I was wondering if I had put my toothbrush in my poncho, I forgot it on our last trip."

Miss Amesbury laughed and said, "You funny child," and thought her more entertaining than ever.

Up beyond Camp Altamont lay a number of small islands and beyond these the river began to bend and twist in numerous eccentric curves; the woods that bordered it grew denser, the banks swampy. Signs of human occupation disappeared; there were no more camps; no more cottages. Great willow trees grew close to the water's edge, five and six trunks coming out of a single root, the drooping branches sweeping the surface of the river. In places rotting logs lay half submerged in the water, looking oddly like alligators in the distance. Usually there would be a turtle sunning himself on the dry end of the log, who craned his neck inquisitively at them as they swept by, as if wondering what strange variety of fish they were. Hinpoha tried to catch one for a mascot, "because he would look so epic tied to the back of our canoe, swimming along behind us," but finally gave it up as a bad job, for none of the turtles seemed to share her enthusiasm over the idea, sinking out of sight at the first preliminaries of adoption. In places the banks, where they were not low and swampy, were perforated like honeycombs with holes some three inches in diameter.

"Oh, what are they?" asked Agony in surprise. "All snake holes?"

"Bank swallows," replied Sahwah. "They make their nests in the mud along river banks that way, until the banks are perfect honeycombs. I don't see how each one knows his own nest; they all look alike to me."

"Maybe they're all numbered in bird language," remarked Miss Amesbury, in her delightfully humorous way.

The scenery grew wilder and wilder as they glided forward and the talk gradually became hushed into a half awed contemplation of the wilderness which closed about them.

"I feel as if I were on some great exploring expedition," exclaimed Sahwah. "Everything looks so new and undiscovered. I wish there was something left to discover," she continued plaintively. "It's so discouraging to think that there's nothing more for explorers to do in this country. What fun it must have been for La Salle and Pere Marquette and Lewis and Clark to find those big rivers that no white man had ever seen before, and go poking about in the wilderness. That was the great and only sport; everything else is tame and flat beside it. I'll never get done envying those early explorers; how I wish I could have been with them!"

"But Sahwah, girls didn't go on long exploring journeys," Gladys interrupted quietly. "They couldn't have borne the hardships."

"Couldn't they?" Sahwah flashed out quickly. "How about Sacajawea, I'd like to know?"

"Goodness, who was she?" asked Gladys.

"The Indian woman who went with Lewis and Clark on their expedition to the Columbia River," replied Sahwah with that tone of animation in her voice which was always present when she spoke of someone whom she admired greatly. "Her husband was the interpreter whom Lewis and Clark took along to talk to the Indians for them, and Sacajawea went with the expedition too, to act as guide, because she knew the Shoshone country. She traveled the whole five thousand miles with them and carried her baby on her back all the while. Lewis and Clark both said afterwards that if it hadn't been for her they wouldn't have been able to make the journey. When there wasn't any meat to eat she knew enough to dig in the prairie dogs' holes for the artichokes which they'd stored up for the winter; and she knew which herbs and berries were fit for food. And on one occasion she saved the most valuable part of the supplies they were carrying, when her stupid husband had managed to upset the boat they were being carried in. While he stood wringing his hands and calling on heaven for help she set to work fishing out the papers and instruments and medicines that had gone overboard, and without which the expedition could not have proceeded. She tramped for hundreds of miles, over hills and through valleys, finding the narrow trails that only the Indians knew, undergoing all the hardships that the men did and never complaining or growing discouraged. On the contrary, she cheered up the men when *they* got discouraged. Now, do you say that a woman can't go exploring as well as a man?"

Sahwah's eyes were sparkling, her cheeks glowed red under their coat of tan, and she was all excitement. The blood of the explorer flowed in her veins; her inheritance from hardy ancestors who had hewn their way through trackless forests to found a new home in the wilderness; and the very mention of exploring set her pulses to leaping wildly. Far back in Sahwah's ancestry there was a strain of Indian blood, which, although it had not been apparent in many of the descendents, had seemed to come into its own in this twentieth century daughter of the Brewsters. Not in looks especially, for Sahwah's hair was brown and not black, and fine and soft as silk, and her features were delicately modeled; yet there was something about her different from the other girls of her acquaintance, something elusive and puzzling, which, for a better name her intimates had called her "Laughing Water" expression. Then, too, there was her passionate love for the woods and for all wild creatures, and the almost uncanny way in which birds and chipmunks would come to her even though they fled in terror at the approach of the other Winnebagos. Was it any wonder that Robert Allison, seeing her for the first time, should have exclaimed involuntarily, "Minnehaha, Laughing Water"?

Thus Sahwah was in her element paddling up this lonely river windingthrough unfamiliar forests, and in her vivid imagination she was Sacajawea, accompanying Lewis and Clark on their famous exploring expedition; and the gentle Onawanda turned into the mighty rolling Columbia, and the friendly pine woods with its border of willows became the trackless forest of the unknown northwest.

Late in the afternoon Jo Severance suddenly cried out, "Here we are!" and called out to the paddlers to head the canoes toward the shore.

Glad to stretch their limbs after the long afternoon of sitting in the canoes, the Winnebagos sprang out on to the rocks which lined the water's edge, and drew the boats up after them. The place was, as Jo had promised, seemingly made for them to camp in. High and dry above the stream, sheltered by great towering pine trees, covered with a thick carpet of pine needles, this little woodland chamber opened in the dense tangle of underbrush which everywhere else grew up between the trees in a heavy tangle. Down near the shore a clear little spring went tinkling down into the river.

"Oh, what a cozy, cozy place!" exclaimed Migwan. "I never thought of being cozy in the woods before - it's always been so wide and airy. This is like your own bedroom, screened in this way with the bushes."

"We'd better get the ponchos unrolled and the beds made up before we start supper," said Sahwah briskly, getting down to business immediately, as usual. The others agreed with alacrity, for they were ravenously hungry from the long paddle and anxious to get at supper as soon as possible.

When they came to lay the ponchos down, however, there was something in the way. The whole narrow plot of smooth ground where they had expected to lay them was covered with evening primroses in full blossom, the fragile yellow blooms standing there so trustfully that they aroused the sympathy of the Winnebagos.

"It's such a pity to crush them under the beds," said tender hearted Migwan. "I'm sure I couldn't sleep if I knew I was killing such brave little things."

The other Winnebagos stood around with their ponchos in their arms, uncertain what to do, loath to be the death of these cheery little wild things, yet unable to see how they could help it.

"Isn't there some other place where we can camp, Jo," asked Migwan, "and let these blossoms live? It seems such a pity to crush them."

Miss Amesbury turned and looked at Migwan with a keen searching glance which caused her to drop her eyes in sudden embarrassment.

Jo took up Migwan's suggestion readily, though disappointed that they were not to stay in her favorite place. "I think we can find another spot," she said, and moved toward the canoes.

Tired and hungry, but perfectly willing to give up the desired spot to save the flowers, the Winnebagos launched out once more, and after paddling for half a mile found another camping ground equally desirable, though not as cozy as the first had been. There was more room here, and the ponchos were laid down without having to sacrifice any flowers.

The sun had set prematurely behind a high bank of gray clouds during the last paddle up the river and there were no rosy sunset glows to reflect on the water and diffuse light into the woods, where a grey twilight had already fallen. There was enough driftwood along the shore to build the fires, and these were soon shining out cheerily through the gathering gloom, while an appetizing odor of coffee and frying bacon filled the air.

The girls lingered long around the fire after supper listening to Miss Amesbury telling tales of her various travels until one by one the logs fell apart and glimmered out into blackness. "And now," said Miss Amesbury, "let's sing one good night song and then roll into bed. We want to be up early in the morning and continue our voyage. There's a heap of 'exploraging' for us to do."

Some time during the night Sahwah was aroused by a gentle pattering noise on her rubber poncho. "It's raining!" she exclaimed to Hinpoha, her sleeping partner.

Hinpoha stirred and murmured drowsily and immediately lay still again.

"It's raining *hard*!" cried Sahwah, now wide awake.

One by one the others began to realize what was happening, and burrowed down under their ponchos, only to emerge a few moments later half smothered.

"Everybody lie still," called Sahwah, "and keep your blankets covered. Hinpoha and I will go out and bring up canoes for shelters."

As she spoke she reached for her bathing suit, which was down under the poncho, and wriggled into it. Hinpoha, still half asleep, but mechanically obeying Sahwah's energetic directions, got into her bathing suit and wriggled out of the bed, drawing the poncho up over her pillow and blankets.

The two sped down to the shore, where the canoes were drawn up on the rocks, and hastily turning one over sideways and packing all their provisions under it, they carried the other two back to the camping ground and inverted them over the head-ends of the beds, their ends propped up on stones, where, tilted back at an angle which shed the water off backward, they made an admirable shelter. Underneath these solid umbrellas the pillows of the girls were as dry as though indoors, and the ponchos protected the blankets. Let the rain come down as hard as it liked, these babes in the wood were snug and warm. As though accepting their challenge to get them wet, the drops came thicker and faster, until they pounded down in a perfect torrent, making a merry din on the canoes as they fell.

"It sounds as if they were saying, 'We'll get you yet, we'll get you yet, we'll get you yet,'" exclaimed Migwan.

Sahwah and Hinpoha, snugly rolled in once more, began to sing "How dry I am." The others took it up, and soon the woods rang with the taunting song of the Winnebagos to the Rain Bird, who replied with a heavier gush than ever. Thunder began to crash overhead, lightning flashed all about them, the great pines tossed and roared like the sea. But the Winnebagos, undismayed, made merry over the storm, and gradually dropped off to sleep again, lulled by the pattering of the raindrops.

In the morning the rain was still falling, rather to their dismay, for they had expected that the storm would soon pass over. The thunder and lightning had ceased, the wind had subsided, and the rain had turned into a steady downpour that looked as if it meant to last all day.

"We'll have to find or build a shelter," remarked Sahwah, thrusting her head, turtle like, from under the edge of the canoe and scanning the heavens with a calculating eye. "This is a regular three days' rain. Who wants to come with me and see if we can find a cave? I have an idea there must be one among the rocks on the hillside just farther on. Who wants to come with me?"

"I'll come!" cried Hinpoha and Jo and Agony and Katherine all in a breath. Cramped from lying still so long, they welcomed the prospect of exercise, even in the early morning rain.

Leaving Migwan and Gladys to keep Miss Amesbury company, the five set out into the streaming woods, and Katherine and Hinpoha and Sahwah came back half an hour later to report that they had found a cave and Jo and Agony had stayed there to build a fire.

"Fire, that sounds good to me," remarked Gladys, shivering a little as she got into her damp bathing suit and drew her heavy sweater over it.

Carrying the beds, still wrapped up in the ponchos, the little procession wound through the woods under the guidance of the returned scouts. The guides were not needed long, however, for soon a heart warming odor of frying bacon came to meet them, and with a world-old instinct each one followed her nose toward it.

"Did anything ever smell so good?" exclaimed Hinpoha, breathing in the fragrant air in long drawn sniffs.

"Those blessed angels!" was all Miss Amesbury could say.

A moment later they stepped out of the wet woods into the cheeriest scene imaginable. In the side of a steep hill which rose not far from the river there opened a good sized cave, and just inside its doorway burned a bright fire, lighting up the interior with its ruddy glow. On a smaller fire beside it a pan of bacon was sizzling merrily, and over another hung a pot of steaming coffee. To the eyes of the wet, chilly campers, it was the most beautiful scene they had ever looked upon. They sprang to the

Hildegard G. Frey

large fire and toasted themselves in its grateful warmth while they held up their clothes to dry before putting them on.

"Thoughtful people, to build us an extra fire," said Miss Amesbury, stretching out luxuriously on the blanket Migwan had spread for her.

"We knew you'd want to warm up a bit," replied Agony, removing the coffee pot from the blaze and beginning to pour the steaming liquid into the cups.

"How did you ever make a fire at all?" inquired Miss Amesbury. "Every bit of wood must be soaked through."

"We dug down into a big pine stump," replied Agony, "or rather, Sahwah did, for I didn't know enough to, and got us some dry chips to start the fire with, and then we kept drying other pieces until they could burn. Once we got that big log started we were all right. It's as hot as a furnace."

"What a difference fire does make!" said Miss Amesbury. "What dreary, dispirited people we'd be by this time if it were not for this cheering blaze. I'd be perfectly content to stay here all day if I had to."

Miss Amesbury had ample opportunity to test the depth of her content, for the rain showed no sign of abating. Hour after hour it poured down steadily as though it had forgotten how to stop. A dense mist rose on the river which gradually spread through the woods until the trees loomed up like dim spectres standing in menacing attitudes before the door of their little rocky chamber. Warm and dry inside, the Winnebagos made the best of their unexpected situation and whiled away the hours with games, stories, and "improving conversation," as Jo Severance recounted later.

"I've just invented a new game," announced Migwan, when the talk had run for some time on famous women of various times.

"What is it?" asked Hinpoha, pausing with a half washed potato in her hand. Hinpoha and Gladys were putting the potatoes into the hot ashes to bake them for dinner.

"Why, it's this," said Migwan. "Let each one of us in turn tell some incident that took place in the girlhood of a famous woman, the one we admire the most, and see if the others can guess who she is."

"All right, you begin, Migwan," said Sahwah.

"No, you begin, Sahwah. It's my game, so I'll be last."

Sahwah sat chin in hand for a moment, and then she began: "I see a long, low house built of bark and branches, thickly covered with snow. It is one of the 'long houses', or winter quarters of the Algonquins, and none other than the Chief's own house. Inside is a council chamber and in it a pow-wow of chiefs is going on. The other half of the house, which is not used as a council chamber, is used as the living room by the family, and here a number of children are playing a lively game. In the midst of the racket the door opens and in comes one of the chief's runners. As he advances toward the council chamber a young girl comes whirling down the room turning handsprings. Her feet strike him full in the chest, and send him flat on his back on the floor. A great roar of laughter goes up from the braves and squaws sitting around the room, for the girl who has knocked the runner down is none other than the chief's own daughter. But the old chief says sadly, 'Why will you be such a tomboy, my child?'"

"Tomboy, tomboy!" cry all the others, using the Algonquin word for that nickname. "Who is my girl, and what is her nickname?"

"That's easy," laughed Migwan, "Who but Pocahontas?"

"Was 'Pocahantas' just a nickname?" asked Hinpoha curiously.

Hildegard G. Frey

"Yes," replied Migwan. "'Pocahontas', or 'pocahuntas', is the Algonquin word for 'tomboy'. The real name of Powhatan's daughter was Ma-ta-oka, but she was known ever after the incident Sahwah just related as 'Pocahontas.'"

"I never heard of that incident," said Hinpoha, "but I might have guessed that Sahwah would take Pocahontas for hers."

"Now you, Agony," said Migwan.

"I see a young girl," began Agony, "tending her flocks in the valley of the Meuse. She is sitting under a large beech, which the children of the village have named the 'Fairy Tree.' As she sits there her face takes on a rapt look; she sits very still, like one in a trance, for her eyes are looking upon a remarkable sight. She seems to see a shining figure standing before her; an angel with a flaming sword. She falls upon her knees and covers her face with her hands, and when she looks up again the vision is gone and only the tree is left, with the church beyond it."

"Joan of Arc!" cried three or four voices at once.

"O, *how* I wish I were she!" finished Agony fervently. "What a life of excitement she must have led! Think of the stirring times she must have had in the army!"

"I envy her all but the stake; I couldn't have borne that," said Sahwah. "Now you, Gladys."

"I see a young English girl, fourteen years old, dressed in the costume of Tudor England, stealing out of Westminster Palace with the boy king of England, Edward the Sixth. Free from the tiresome lords and ladies-in-waiting who were always at their heels in the palace, they have a gorgeous time wandering about the streets of London until by chance they meet one of the royal household, and are hustled back to the palace in short order."

"Poor Lady Jane Grey!" said Migwan. "I'm glad I wasn't in her shoes. I'm glad I'm not in any royalty's shoes. With all their pomp and splendor they never have half the fun we're having at this minute," she continued vehemently. "They never went off on a hike by themselves and slept on the ground with their heads under a canoe. It's lots nicer to be free, even if you *are* a nobody."

"I think so too," Sahwah agreed with her emphatically.

"My girl," said Jo, in her turn, "was crowned queen at the age of nine months and betrothed to the King of France when she was five years old. That's all I know about her early days, except that she had four intimate friends all named Mary."

"Mary, Queen of Scots," guessed Gladys, who was taking a history course in college. "Somehow I never could get up much sympathy for her; she seemed such a spineless sort of creature. I always preferred Queen Elizabeth, even if she did cut off Mary's head."

"Every single one of the heroines so far has died a violent death," remarked Miss Amesbury. "Is that the only kind of women you admire?"

"It seems so," replied Migwan, laughing. "We're a bloodthirsty lot. Go on, Katherine."

Katherine dropped the log she was carrying upon the fire and kept her eye upon it as she spoke. "I see a brilliant assemblage, gathered in the palace of the Empress of Austria to hear a wonderful boy musician play on the piano. As the young lad, who is none other than the great Mozart, enters the room, he first approaches the Empress to make his bow to her. The polished floor is extremely slippery, and he slips and falls flat. The courtiers, who consider him very clumsy, do nothing but laugh at him, but the young daughter of the Empress runs forward, helps him to his feet and comforts him with soothing words."

"I always did think that was the most charming anecdote ever related about Marie Antoinete," observed Migwan. "She must have been a very sweet and lovable young girl; it doesn't seem possible that she grew up to be the kind of woman she did."

"Another one who lost her head!" remarked Miss Amesbury, laughing. "Aren't there going to be any who live to grow old? Let's see who Hinpoha's favorite heroine is."

Hinpoha moved back a foot or so from the fire, which had blazed up to an uncomfortable heat at the addition of Katherine's log. "I see a Puritan maiden, seated at a spinning wheel," she commenced. "The door opens and a young man comes in. He apparently has something on his mind, and stands around first on one foot and then on the other, until the girl asks him what seems to be the trouble, whereupon he gravely informs her that a friend of his, a most worthy man indeed, who can write, and fight, and - ah, do several more things all at once, wants her for his wife. Then the girl smiles demurely at him, and says coyly -"

"Why don't you speak for yourself, John?" shouted the other six girls, with one voice.

"You don't need to ask Hinpoha who her favorite heroine is," said Migwan laughing. "Ever since I've known her she's read the story of Priscilla and John Alden at least once a week."

"Well, you must admit that she *was* pretty clever," said Hinpoha, blushing a little at the exposure of her fondness for love stories. "And sensible, too. She wasn't afraid of speaking up and helping her bashful lover along a little bit, instead of meekly accepting Standish's offer and then spending the rest of her life sighing because John Alden hadn't asked her."

"That's right," chimed in Sahwah. "I admire a girl with spirit. If Lady Jane Gray had had a little more spirit she wouldn't have lost her head. I'll warrant Priscilla Mullins would have found a way out of it if she had been in the same scrape as

Lady Jane. Now, your turn, Migwan."

"I see a girl living in a bleak house on the edge of a wild, lonely moor," began Migwan. "All winter long the storms howl around the house like angry spirits of the air. To amuse themselves in these long winter evenings this girl and her sisters make up stories about the people that live on the moors and tell them to each other around the fire, or after they have crept into bed, and lie shivering under the blankets in the icy cold room. The stories that my girl made up were so fascinating that the others forgot the cold and the raw winds whistling about the house and listened spellbound until she had finished."

"I know who that is," said Gladys, when Migwan paused. "Mig is forever raving about Charlotte Bronte."

"The more I think about her the more wonderful she seems," said Migwan warmly. "How a girl brought up in such a dead, cheerless place as Haworth Churchyard, and knowing nothing at all about the world of people, could have written such a book as *Jane Eyre*, seems a miracle. She was a genius," she finished with an envious sigh.

Miss Amesbury looked keenly at Migwan. "I think," she observed shrewdly, "that you like to write also. Is it not so?"

Migwan blushed furiously and sat silent. To have this successful, widely known writer know her heart's ambition filled her with an agony of embarrassment.

"Migwan does write, wonderful things," said Hinpoha loyally. "She's had things printed in papers and in the college magazine." Then she told about the Indian legend that had caused such a stir in college, whereupon Miss Amesbury laughed heartily, and patted Migwan on the head, and said she would very much like to see some of the things she had written. Migwan, thrilled and happy, but still very much embarrassed, shyly promised that she would let her see some of her work, and in the middle of her speech a potato blew up with a bang, showering them all with mealy fragments and hot ashes, and sending them flying away from the fire with startled shrieks.

Since the potatoes were so very evidently done, the rest of the meal was hurriedly prepared, and eaten with keen appetites. During the clearing away process somebody discovered that the rain had stopped falling, a fact which they had all been too busy to notice before, and that the mist was being rapidly blown away by a strong northwest wind. When they woke in the morning, after sleeping in the cave around the fire, the sun was shining brightly into the entrance and the birds outside were singing joyously of a fair day to come.

Overflowing with energy the late cave dwellers raced through the sweet smelling woods, indescribably fresh and fragrant after the cleansing, purifying rain, and launched the canoes upon a river Sparkling like a sheet of diamonds in the clear morning sunlight. How wonderfully new and bright the rain-washed earth looked everywhere, and how exhilarating the fresh rushing wind was to their senses, after the smoky, misty atmosphere of the cave!

Exulting in their strength the Winnebagos bent low over their paddles, and the canoes leaped forward like hounds set free from the leash, and went racing along with the current, shooting past islands, whirling around bends, whisking through tiny rapids, wildly, deliriously, rejoicing in the thrill of the morning and the call of a world running over with joy. Soon they came to the place where they had first planned to camp, and there were the primroses, a-riot with bloom, nodding them a friendly greeting.

"Aren't you glad we didn't stay here?" said Sahwah. "We'd have been soaked if we did, because we probably wouldn't have found the cave. The primroses saved the day for us by growing where we wanted to lay our beds."

They sang a cheer to the primroses and swept on until they came to the place in the woods where the balsam grew. Dusk was falling when, with canoes piled high with the fragrant boughs, they rounded the great bend above Keewaydin and a few minutes later ran in alongside the Camp Keewaydin dock.

"I feel as though I had been gone for weeks," said Migwan, as they climbed out of the canoes.

"So do I," said Sahwah, dancing up and down on the dock to take the stiffness out of her muscles. "Doesn't it look civilized, though, after what we've just experienced? I wish," she continued longingly, "that I could live in the wilds all the time."

"I don't," replied Migwan, patting the diving tower as if it were an old friend. "Camp is plenty wild enough for me."

Hildegard G. Frey

CHAPTER X

TOPSY-TURVY DAY

"Why, where *is* camp?" asked Sahwah in perplexity, noticing that the whole place was dark and still. It was half past six, the usual after-supper frolic hour, when camp was wont to ring to the echo with fun and merriment of all kinds. Now no sound came from Mateka, nor from the bungalow, nor from any of the tents, no sound and no movement. Before their astonished eyes the camp lay like an enchanted city, changed in their absence from a place of racket and bustle and resounding laughter, to a silent ghost of its former lively self.

"What's happened?" exclaimed the Winnebagos to each other. "Is everybody gone on a trip?"

Mystified, they climbed up the hill, and at the top they found Miss Judy going from tent to tent with her flashlight, as if making the nightly rounds after lights out.

"O Miss Judy," they called to her, "what's happened?"

"Shh-h-h!" replied Miss Judy, holding up her hand for silence and coming toward them. "Everybody's in bed," she whispered when she was near enough for them to hear her."

"In bed!" exclaimed the Winnebagos in astonishment. "At half past six in the evening? What for?"

"It's Topsy-Turvy Day," replied Miss Judy, laughing at their amazed faces. "We're turning everything upside down tonight. Hurry and get into bed. The rising bugle will blow in half an hour."

Giggling with amusement the Winnebagos sped to their tents, unrolled their ponchos, made up their beds in a hurry, undressed quickly and popped into bed. Not long afterward they heard the dipping of paddles and the monotonous "one, two, one two," of the boatswain as the crew of the Turtle started out for practice. The Turtle's regular practice hour was the half hour before rising bugle in the morning.

Tired with her long paddle that day Hinpoha fell asleep as soon as she touched the pillow, and was much startled to hear the loud blast of a bugle in the midst of a delightful dream. "What's the matter?" she asked sleepily, sitting up and looking around her in bewilderment. "What are they blowing the bugle in the middle of the night for?"

"They aren't blowing the bugle in the middle of the night," said Sahwah with a shriek of laughter at Hinpoha's puzzled face. "This is Topsy-Turvy Day, don't you remember? We're going to have our regular day's program at night time. It's ten minutes to seven, and that's the bugle for morning dip. Are you coming?"

Sahwah was already inside her bathing suit, and Agony had hers half on. Hinpoha replied with an unintelligible sound, one-eighth grunt and seven-eights yawn, and rising tipsily from her bed she looked around for her bathing suit with eyes still half sealed by sleep. Sahwah helped her into the suit and seizing her hand led her down to the water, where half the camp, shaking with convulsive merriment at the absurdity of the thing, were scrupulously taking their "morning dip," with toothbrush drill and all the other regular morning ablutions.

The rising bugle blew while they were still at it and they sped back to the tents to get dressed, making three times as much racket about this process as they ever did in the morning. Most of the tents had no lights, because ordinarily no one needed a light to undress by and so the lanterns which had been given out at the beginning of the season were scattered everywhere about camp as especial need for them had arisen upon various occasions. But getting dressed in the dark is harder than getting undressed, and most of the tents were in an uproar.

"I can only find one stocking," wailed Oh-Pshaw, after vainly feeling around for several minutes. "Where's my flashlight, Katherine?"

"I'm sorry, but I just dropped it into the water jar," replied Katherine, "and it won't work any more." Katherine herself was hopelessly involved in her bloomers, having put both feet through the same leg, and was lying flat on the floor trying to extricate herself.

"Can I go with only one stocking on?" Oh-Pshaw persisted plaintively. "I haven't another pair here in the tent."

"*I* can't find my middy," Jean Lawrence was lamenting, paying no heed to Oh-Pshaw's troubles in regard to hosiery.

Tiny Armstrong, reaching down behind her bed for some missing article of her costume, gave the bed such a shove that it went flying out of the tent carrying the rustic railing with it, and they heard it go bumping down the hillside.

"Strike one!" called Tiny ruefully. "That's what comes of being so strong. I'll knock the tent down next."

"Will somebody please tell me where my middy is?" Jean cried tragically. "I can't find it anywhere."

"Will someone tell *me* where the other leg of my bloomers is?" exclaimed Katherine. "I've shoved both feet through the same leg three times, now. There goes the breakfast bugle!"

"Oh, where is my other stocking?"

"Where is my middy?"

"Who's gone south with my shoes?"

The threefold wail floated down on the breeze as footsteps began to run down the Alley in the direction of the bungalow. A few minutes later the occupants of Bedlam slid as unobtrusively as possible into the lighted bungalow; Oh-Pshaw with her bloomers down around her ankles in a Turkish effect, to hide the fact that she had on only one stocking; Jean with her sweater buttoned tightly around her, Katherine with her red silk tie bound around one knee to gather up the fullness of her bloomer leg, for the elastic band had burst from the strain of accommodating two feet at once; and Tiny had one white sneaker and one red Pullman slipper on. Glancing around at the rest they saw many others in the same plight - middies on hindside before, odd shoes and stockings, sweaters instead of middies, and various other parodies on the regular camp uniform - and immediately they ceased to feel conspicuous. Taking their places around the table the campers proceeded to sing one of the morning greetings:

"Good morning to you,
Good morning to you,
Good morning, dear comrades,
Good morning to you!"

"Did you have a good night's sleep?" was a question that made the rounds of the table, with many droll replies, as the cereal was being passed. Hilarity increased during the meal, as the absurdity of eating cereal and fruit and toast at eight o'clock in the evening overcame the girls one after the other, and the room rang with witty songs made up on the spur of the moment.

At "Morning Sing" which followed breakfast, they solemnly sang "When Morning Gilds the Skies," "Awake, my soul, and with the sun," "Kathleen Mavourneen, the grey dawn is breaking," and other morning songs; the program for the day was read, and Dr. Grayson gave a fatherly lecture on the harmfulness of staying up after dark. Getting the tents ready for tent inspection without lights was a proceeding which defies description. Tiny Armstrong was still on the hillside searching for her runaway bed when the Lone Wolf reached Bedlam in her tour of inspection, and was given a large and black zero in consequence. She finally gave up the search and wandered into Mateka, where, with lanterns hanging above the long tables, Craft Hour was in full swing, the girls busily working at clay modeling, wood-blocking and paddle decorating, while the moon, round-eyed with astonishment, peeped through the doorway at the singular sight. Still more astonished, the same moon looked down on the tennis court an hour later, where a lively folk dance was going on to the music of a graphaphone; couples spinning around in wild figures, stepping on each other's feet and every now and then dropping down at the outer edge of the court and shrieking with laughter, while the dance continued faster and more furiously than before till the sound of the bugle sent the dancers flying swiftly to their tents to wriggle into clammy, wet bathing suits that seemed in the dark to be an altogether different shape from what they were in the daylight.

Standing on top of the diving tower when Tiny's cry of "All in!" rang out, Sahwah leaped down into the darkness and had a queer, thrilling moment in mid air when she wondered if she would ever strike the water, or would go on indefinitely falling through the blackness. Laughing, shouting, splashing, the campers sported in the water until all of a sudden a red canoe shot into their midst and the director of Camp Altamont, accompanied by two assistants, came in an advanced stage of breathlessness to find out what the matter was. They heard the noise and the splashing of water and thought some accident had occurred.

"No accident, thanks, only Camp Keewaydin stealing a march on old Father Time and turning night into day," Dr. Grayson called from the dock, and amid shouts of laughter from all around the messengers paddled back to their camp to assure the wakened and excited boys that nothing had happened, and that it was only another wild inspiration of the people at Camp Keewaydin.

At midnight, when the bugle blew for dinner, everyone was as hungry as at noon, and the kettle of cocoa and the trays of sandwiches were emptied in a jiffy.

"Now what?" asked Dr. Grayson, looking around the table with twinkling eyes, when the last crumb and the last drop of cocoa had disappeared.

"Rest hour," replied Mrs. Grayson emphatically. "Rest hour to last until morning. Blow the bugle, Judy."

"Wasn't this the wildest evening we ever put in?" said Katherine, fishing her hairbrush out of the water pail. "Where's Tiny?" she asked, becoming aware that their Councilor was not in the tent,

"Down on the hill looking for her bed." replied Oh-Pshaw.

"Goodness, let's go down and help her," said Katherine, and Oh-Pshaw and Jean streamed after her down the path. They stumbled over the bed before they came to Tiny. It had turned over sidewise and fallen into a tiny ravine, and as she had gone straight down the hill searching for it she had missed it. Katherine stepped into the ravine, dragging the two others with her, and at the bottom they landed on top of the bed.

Getting an iron cot up a steep hill is not the easiest thing in the world, and when they had it up at the top of the hill they all sat down on it and panted awhile before they could make it up. Then they discovered that the pillow was missing and Katherine obligingly went down the hill again to find it.

"I shan't get up again for a week," she sighed wearily as she stretched between the sheets.

"Neither will I, ' echoec Tiny.

Jean and Oh-Pshaw did not echo. They were already asleep.

Katherine had just sunk into a deep slumber when she started at the touch of a cold hand laid against her face. "What is it?" she cried out sharply.

A face was bending over her, a pale little face framed in a lace boudoir cap. Katherine recognized Carmen Chadwick. "What's the matter?" she asked.

"My Councy's awful sick, and none of the other girls will wake up and I don't know what to do," said Carmen in a scared voice.

"What's the matter with her?" asked Katherine.

"She ate too many blueberries, I guess; she's got an awful pain in her stomach and chills."

Katherine hugged her warm pillow. "Take the hot water bottle out of the washstand," she directed, without moving. "There - it's on the top shelf. There's hot water in the tank in the kitchen. And have you some Jamaica ginger? No? Take ours - it's the only bottle on the top shelf. Now you'll be all right."

Katherine sank back into slumber. A few minutes more and she was awakened again by the same cold hand on her face.

"What is it now?"

"The Jamaica ginger." asked Carmen's thin voice in a bewildered tone, "what shall I do with it? Shall I put it in the hot water bottle?"

Katherine's feet suddenly struck the floor together, and with an explosive exclamation under her breath she sped over to Avernus and took matters in hand herself. She had tucked Carmen into her own bed in Bedlam, and she spent the remainder of the night over in Avernus, taking care of the Lone Wolf, snatching a few moments' sleep in Carmen's bed now and then when her patient felt easier. It was broad daylight before she finally settled into uninterrupted slumber.

CHAPTER XI

EDWIN LANGHAM

Camp was more or less demoralized the next day. Miss Judy overslept and did not blow the rising bugle until nearly noon, so dinner took the place of breakfast and swimming hour came in the middle of the afternoon instead of in the morning.

After swimming hour Agony went up to Miss Amesbury's balcony to return a book she had borrowed. Miss Amesbury was not there, so Agony, as she often did when she found her friend out, sat down to wait for her, passing the time by looking at some sketches tying on the table. Turing these over, Agony came upon a letter thrust in between the drawing sheets, at the sight of which her heart began to flutter wildly. The address on the envelope was in Mary Sylvester's handwriting - there was no mistaking that firm, round hand; it was indelibly impressed upon Agony's mind from seeing it on that other occasion. In a panic she realized that the danger of being discovered was even greater than she had thought, since Mary also wrote to Miss Amesbury. Was it not possible that Mary had mentioned the robin incident in this letter? It now seemed to Agony that Miss Amesbury's manner had been different toward her in the last few days, on the trip. She seemed less friendly, less cordial. Several times Agony had looked up lately to find Miss Amesbury regarding her with a keen, grave scrutiny and a baffling expression on her face. To Agony's tortured fancy these instances became magnified out of all proportion, and the disquieting conviction seized her that Miss Amesbury knew the truth. The thought nearly drove her mad. It tormented her until she realized that there was only one way in which she could still the tumult raging in her bosom, and that was by finding out for certain if Mary had really told.

With shaking fingers she slipped the letter out of the open envelope, and with cheeks aflame with shame at the thing she was doing, she deliberately read Miss Amesbury's letter. It was much like the one Mary had written to Jo Severance, full of clever descriptions of the places she was seeing, and it made no mention either of the robin or of her. With fingers shaking still more at the relief she felt, she put the letter back into the envelope and replaced it between the sketches. Then, trembling from head to foot at the reaction from her panic, she turned her back upon the table and sat up against the railing, holding her head in her hands and looking down at the fair sunlit river with eyes that saw it not.

Miss Amesbury returned by and by and was so evidently pleased to see her that Agony concluded she must have been mistaken in fancying any coldness on her part during the last few days.

"I've a letter from Mary Sylvester," Miss Amesbury said almost at once, "and because you are following so closely in Mary's footsteps I'm going to read it to you." She smiled brightly into Agony's sober face and paused to pat her on the shoulder before she fluttered over the pile of sketches to find the letter.

Agony sat limply, listening to the words she had read a few minutes before, despising herself thoroughly and wishing with all her heart that she had never come to camp. Yet she forced herself to make appreciative comments on the interesting things in the letter and to utter sincere sounding exclamations of surprise at certain points.

"I've something to tell you that will please you," said Miss Amesbury, after the letter had been put away.

"What is it?" asked Agony, looking up inquiringly.

"Someone you admire very much is going to visit Camp," replied Miss Amesbury.

"Who?" Agony's eyes opened up very wide with surprise.

"Edwin Langham. He has been camping not very far from here and he is going to run down on his way home and pay Dr. Grayson a flying visit. They are old friends."

"Edwin Langham?" Agony gasped faintly, her head awhirl. It seemed past comprehension that this man whom she had worshipped as a divinity for so long was actually to materialize in the flesh - that the cherished desire of her life was coming true, that she was going to see and talk with him.

"Goodness, don't look so excited, child," said Miss Amesbury, laughing. "He's only a man. A very rare and wonderful man, however," she added, "and it is a great privilege to know him.'

"When is he coming?" asked Agony in a whisper.

"Tomorrow afternoon. He is going to stop off between boats and will be here only a short time."

"Do you suppose he will speak to me?" asked Agony humbly.

"I rather think he will," replied Miss Amesbury, smiling. "You see," she continued, taking Agony's hand in hers as she spoke, "it just happened that Edwin Langham was the man who sat under the tree that time you climbed up and rescued the robin. He was laid up with blood poisoning in his foot at the time and he had been wheeled into the woods from his camp that afternoon. His man had left him for a short time when you happened along. He was the man who told about the incident down at the store at Green's Landing, where Dr. Grayson heard about it later from the storekeeper. Dr. Grayson did not know at the time that it was his friend Edwin Langham who had witnessed the affair, but in the letter Dr. Grayson has just received from Mr. Langham he gives an enthusiastic account of it, and says he is coming to camp partly for the purpose of meeting the girl in the green bloomers who performed that splendid deed that day. So you see, my dear," Miss Amesbury concluded, "I think it is highly probable that you will have an opportunity to speak to your idolized Edwin Langham."

For a moment things turned black before Agony's eyes. She rose unsteadily to her feet and crossed the balcony to the stairs. "I must be going, now," she murmured through dry lips.

"Must you go so soon?" asked Miss Amesbury with a real regret in her voice that cut Agony to the heart.

"Come again, come often," floated after her as she passed through the door.

Agony sped away from camp and hid herself away in the woods, where she sank down at the foot of a great tree and hid her face in her hands. The thing she had desired, had longed for above all others, was now about to come to pass - and she had made it forever an impossibility. The cup of joy that Fate had decreed she was to taste she had dashed to the ground with her own hands. For she could not see Edwin Langham, could not let him see her. As long as he did not see her her secret was safe. He did not know her name, or Mary's, so he could not betray her in that way. Only, if he ever saw her he would know the difference right away, and then would come betrayal and disgrace. There was only one thing to do. She must hide away from him; and give up her opportunity of meeting and talking with him. It was the only way out of the predicament.

When the steamer swung into view around the bend of the river the next afternoon Agony stole away into the thickest part of the woods and proceeded toward a place she had discovered some time before. It was a deep, extremely narrow ravine, so narrow indeed that it was merely a great crock in the earth, not more than six feet across at its widest. It was filled with a wild growth of elderberry bushes, which made it an excellent hiding place. She scrambled down into this pit and crouched under the bushes, completely hidden from view. Here she sat with her head bowed down on her knees, hearing the whistle of the steamer as it neared the dock, and the welcoming song of the girls as the distinguished passenger alighted. A little later it seemed to her that she heard voices calling her name. Yes, it was so, without a doubt. Tiny Armstrong's megaphone voice came echoing on the breeze.

"A-go-ny! A-go-ny! Oh-h-h-h, A - go - ny!"

*　*　*　*　*

She clenched her hands in silent misery, and did not raise her head. Then the sound of a bark arrested her attention, coming from directly overhead, and she sat up in consternation. Micky, the bull pup belonging to the Camp, had discovered her hiding place and would undoubtedly give her away.

"Go away, Micky!" she commanded in a low tone. At the sound of her voice Micky barked more loudly than ever, a joyous, welcoming bark. Having been much petted by Agony, Micky had grown very fond of her, and seeing her walk off into the woods today, he had followed after her, and now gave loud voice to his satisfaction at finding her.

"Micky! Go away!" commanded Agony a second time, throwing a lump of dirt at him. Micky looked astonished as the dirt flew past his nose, but refused to retire.

"Well, if you won't go away, come down in here, then," said Agony. "Here, Micky, Micky," she called coaxingly.

Micky, clumsy puppy that he was, made a wild leap into the ravine and landed upon the sharp point of a jagged stump, cutting a jagged gash in his shoulder. How he did howl! Agony expected every minute that the whole camp would come running to the spot to find out what the matter was. But fortunately the wind was blowing from the direction of Camp and the sound was carried the other way. Agony worked frantically to get the wound bound up and the poor puppy soothed into silence. At last he lay still, with his head in her lap, licking her hand with his moppy red tongue every few seconds to tell her how grateful he was.

Thus she sat until she heard the deep whistle of the returning steamer and the farewell song of the girls as they stood on the dock and waved goodbye to Edwin Langham. When she was sure that the boat must be out of sight she shoved Micky gently out of her lap and rose to climb out of her hiding place. Her feet were asleep from sitting so long in her cramped position and as she tried to get a foothold on the steep side of the ravine she slipped and fell headlong, striking her head on a stump and twisting her back. It was not until night that they found her, after her continued absence from camp had roused alarm, and searching parties had been made up to scour the woods. Tiny Armstrong, shouting her way through the woods, first heard a muffled bark and then a feeble answer to her call, coming from the direction of the ravine, and charging toward it like a fire engine she discovered the two under the elderberry bushes.

Agony was lifted gently out and laid on the ground to await the coming of an improvised stretcher.

"We hunted and hunted for you this afternoon," said Jo Severance, bending over her with an anxious face. "The poet, Edwin Langham, was here, and he wanted especially to see you, and was dreadfully disappointed when we couldn't find you. He left a book here for you."

"Oh," groaned Agony, and those hearing her thought that she must be in great physical pain.

"How did you happen to fall into that ravine?" asked Jo.

Agony was becoming light headed from the blow on her

temple, and she answered in disjointed phrases.

"Didn't fall in - went down - purpose. Micky - fell in - hurt shoulder - I bandaged it - fell trying - to - get - out."

Her voice trailed off weakly toward the end.

"There, don't talk," said Dr. Grayson. "We understand all about it. The dog fell in and hurt himself and you went down after him and then fell in yourself. Being kind to dumb animals again. Noble little girl. We're proud of you."

Agony heard it all as in a dream, but could summon no voice to speak. She was *so* tired. After all, why not let them think that? It was the best way out. Otherwise they might wonder how she happened to be in the ravine - it would be hard for them to believe that she had fallen into it herself in broad daylight, and it might be embarrassing to answer questions. Let them believe that she had gone down after the dog. That settled the matter once for all.

The stretcher arrived and she was carried to her tent, where Dr. Grayson made a thorough examination of her injuries.

"Not serious," was his verdict, to everybody's immense relief. "Painful bump on the head, but no real damage done, and back strained a little, that's all."

Once more Agony was the camp heroine, and her tent was crowded all day long with admirers. Miss Amesbury sat and read to her by the hour; the camp cook made up special dishes and sent them out on a tray trimmed with wild flowers; the camp orchestra serenaded her daily and nightly, and half a dozen clever camp poets made up songs in her honor. Fame comes easily in camps and enthusiasm runs high while it lasts.

Agony reflected, in a grimly humorous way, that in the matter of fame she had a sort of Midas touch; everything she did rebounded to her glory, now that the ball was once started rolling. And worst of all was the book that Edwin Langham had left for her, a beautiful copy of "The Desert Garden," bound in limp leather with gold edged leaves. Inside the cover was written in a flowing, beautiful hand:

"To A.C.W., in memory of a certain day in the woods.
From one who rejoices in a brave and noble deed.
Sincerely, Edwin Langham."

On the opposite page was written a quotation which Agony had been familiar with ever since she had become a Winnebago:

"Love is the joy of service so deep that self is forgotten."

She put the book away where she could not see it, but the words had burned themselves into her brain.

"To A.C.W. From one who rejoices in a brave and noble deed."

They mocked her in the dead of night, they taunted her in the light of day. But, like the boy with the fox gnawing at his vitals, Agony continued to smile and make herself agreeable, and no one ever suspected that her gayety was not genuine.

CHAPTER XII

THE STUNT'S THE THING

"Where would a shipwreck look best, right by the dock, or farther up the shore?" Sahwah's forehead puckered up with the force of her reflection.

"Oh, not right by the dock," said Jo Severance decidedly. "That would be too modern and - commonplace. It's lots more epic to be dashed against a rocky cliff. All the shipwrecks in the books happen on stern and rockbound coasts and things like that."

"It might be more epic for those who are looking on, but for the one that gets shipwrecked," Sahwah reminded her. "As long as I'm the one that get's wrecked I'm going to pick out a soft spot to get wrecked on."

"Why not capsize some distance out in the water and swim ashore?" suggested Migwan.

"Of course!" exclaimed Sahwah. "Why didn't we think of that before? Geese!"

"This is the way we'll start, then," said Migwan, taking out her notebook and scribbling in it with a pencil. "Scene One. Sinbad the Sailor clinging to wreckage of vessel out in the water. He drifts ashore and lands in the kingdom of the Keewaydins." She paused and bit the end of her pencil, seeking inspiration. "Then, what will you do when you land, Sahwah?"

"Oh, I'll just poke around a bit, and then discover the Keewaydins in their native wilds," replied Sahwah easily. "Then I'll go around with you while you go through the events of a day in camp. O, I think it's the grandest idea!" she interrupted herself in a burst of rapture. "We'll get the stunt prize as easy as pie. The Avenue will never be able to think up anything nearly as good. How did you ever manage to think of it, Migs?"

"Why, it just came all by itself," replied Migwan modestly.

Anyone who had ever spent a summer at Camp Keewaydin, passing at that moment, and hearing the conversation, would have known exactly what week of the year it was without consulting a calendar. It was the second week in August - the week of Camp Keewaydin's annual Stunt Night, when the Avenue and the Alley matched their talents in a contest to see which one could put on the best original stunt. Next to Regatta Day, when the two struggled for the final supremacy in aquatics, Stunt Night was the biggest event of the camping season. Rivalry was intense. It was a fair test of the talents of the girls themselves, for the councilors were not allowed to participate, nor to give the slightest aid or advice. The boys from Camp Altamont came over with their councilors, and together with the directors and councilors of Camp Keewaydin they voted on which stunt was the best. Originality counted most; finish in working out the details next.

The Alley's stunt this year was a sketch entitled THE LAST VOYAGE OF SINBAD THE SAILOR, and was a burlesque on Camp life. The idea had come to Migwan in a flash of inspiration one night when Dr. Grayson was reading the Arabian Nights aloud before the fire in the bungalow. She communicated her idea to the rest of the Alley and they received it with whoops of joy.

Now it lacked but three days until Stunt Night, and the

Alleyites, over on Whaleback, where they would be safe from detection, were deep in the throes of rehearsing. Sahwah, of course, was picked for the role of the shipwrecked Sinbad, for she was the only one who could be depended upon to stage the shipweck in a thrilling manner.

"What kind of a costume do I wear?" she inquired, when the location of the shipwreck itself had finally been settled. "What nationality was Sinbad, anyhow?"

"He came from Bagdad," replied Sahwah brilliantly.

"But where was Bagdad?"

"In Syria," declared Oh-Pshaw.

"Asia," promptly answered Gladys.

"Turkey," said Katherine, somewhat doubtfully, and "Persia," said Agony in the same breath.

Then they all looked at each other a little sheepishly.

"The extent to which I don't know geography," remarked Sahwah, "is something appalling."

"Well, if *we* don't know what country Bagdad was in, it's pretty sure that none of the others will either," said Hinpoha brightly, "so it doesn't make much difference what kind of a costume you wear. Something Turkish is what you want, I suppose. A turban and some great big bloomers, you know the kind, with yards and yards of goods in them."

"But you can't swim in such awfully full bloomers," Sahwah protested.

"That's so, too," Hinpoha assented.

"Well, get them as big as you *can* swim in," said

Migwan pacifically.

"Who's going to make them?" Sahwah wanted to know. "We haven't much time."

"Oh, just borrow Tiny Armstrong's regular ones," Migwan replied. "They'll look like Turkish bloomers on you."

"Won't she suspect what we're going to do if I borrow them?" Sahwah demurred.

"Nonsense! What could she suspect? She will know of course that you want them for the stunt, but she couldn't guess *what* for."

"We've got to have her other pair, too, for the person who is going to impersonate Tiny," Agony reminded Migwan.

"So we do," replied Migwan, making a note in her book. "And her stockings, too, those red and black ones. We're going to do that snake business over again. Somebody will have to get these without Tiny's knowing it, or she'll suspect about the snake. Who's in her tent?"

"We are," replied Katherine and Oh-Pshaw. "We'll manage to get them for you. Who's going to impersonate Tiny Armstrong?"

Migwan squinted her eyes in a calculating manner and surveyed the girls grouped around her. "It'll have to be Katherine, I guess," she finally announced. "She's the biggest of us all. But even she isn't nearly as big as Tiny," she added regretfully.

"Couldn't we put two of us together?" suggested Sahwah. "Carmen Chadwick is as light as a feather and she could get up on Katherin's shoulders as easy as not."

"But we need Katherine to impersonate the Lone Wolf. She's

the only one who can do it well," objected Migwan. "Somebody else will have to be the bottom half of Tiny. Hinpoha, you'll do for that part. Gladys, you'll be Pom-pom, of course. There, that's three councilors taken care of. As soon as your parts are assigned will you please step over to that side, girls. Then I can see what I have left. Now, who'll be Miss Peckham?"

There was a silence, and all the eligibles looked at one another doubtfully. Nobody quite dared impersonate Miss Peckham - and nobody wanted to, for that matter.

"Jo?" Migwan began hesitatingly. "You're such a good mimic - no -" she broke off decidely, "you have to be Dr. Grayson, of course, because you can play men's parts so beautifully."

She looked from one to the other inquiringly. Her eye fell upon Bengal Virden. 'Bengal, dear -"

Bengal looked up with a jerk and a grimace of distaste. "I wouldn't be Pecky for a thousand dollars," she declared flatly. "I hate her, I tell you." Then something seemed to occur to her, and a mischievous twinkle came into her eyes. "Oh, I'll be her," she exclaimed, throwing grammar to the winds in her eagerness. "Please let me. I want to be, I want to be."

"All right," said Migwan relievedly, putting the entry down in her notebook and proceeding with the assignment of parts. But Agony, having seen the mischievous gleam that came into Bengal's eyes when she so suddenly changed her mind about impersonating Miss Peckham, wondered as to its meaning.

She called Bengal to come aside with her, and Bengal, enraptured at being noticed by her divinity, trotted after her like a delighted Newfoundland puppy, bestowing clumsy caresses upon her as they proceeded.

"Oh, I've got the best joke on Pecky!" she gurgled, before Agony had had a chance to broach the subject herself.

"Yes?" said Agony.

"Did you know," confided Bengal, with a fresh burst of giggles, "that Pecky shaves?"

Then, as Agony gave a little incredulous exclamation, she hastened on. "Really she does, her whole chin, with a razor, every morning. I found it out a couple of days ago. I guess she'd have a regular beard if she didn't. You've noticed how kind of hairy her chin is, haven't you? I found a little safety razor among her things one day -"

"Bengal! You weren't rummaging among her things, were you?"

"No, of course not. But once when we were all up in the bungalow she found that she'd forgotten her watch, and sent me back to get it out of her bathrobe pocket, and there was a little safety razor in where the watch was. I didn't think anything about it then, but after that I noticed that she always went off by herself in the woods. While the rest of us went for morning dip. Yesterday I followed her and saw what she did. She shaved her chin with that safety razor. Oh, won't it be great fun when I do that in the stunt? Won't she be hopping mad, though!" Bengal hopped up and down and chortled with anticipatory glee.

"Bengal!" said Agony firmly, "don't you *dare* do anything like that? Don't you know that it's terribly bad taste to make fun of people's personal blemishes?"

"But she deserves it," Bengal persisted, still chuckling. "She's such a prune."

"That has nothing whatever to do with the matter," Agony replied sternly. "Do you want to ruin our stunt for us? That's what will happen if you do anything as ill-bred as that. It would take away every chance we have of winning the prize."

"Well, if *you* say I shouldn't do it I won't," said Bengal rather sulkily. "But wouldn't it have been the best joke!" she added regretfully.

"Bengal," Agony continued, realizing that even if Bengal could be suppressed as far as the stunt went, she would still have plenty of opportunity for making life miserable for Miss Peckham now that she had learned her embarrassing secret, "you won't mention this to any of the other girls, will you? You see, it must be very embarrassing for Miss Peckham to have to do that, and naturally she would feel highly uncomfortable if the camp found it out. You see, you found it out by accident; she didn't tell you of her own free will, so you have no right to tell it any further. A girl with a nice sense of honor would never think of telling anything she found out in that way, when she knew it would cause embarrassment if told. So you'll give me your promise, won't you, Bengal dear, that you will never mention this matter to anybody around camp?"

Bengal flushed and looked down, maintaining an obstinate silence.

"Please, won't you, Bengal dear?" coaxed Agony in her most irresistible manner. "Will you do it for me if you won't do it for Miss Peckham?"

Bengal could not hold out against the coaxing of her adored one, but she still hesitated, bargaining her promise for a reward. "If you'll let me wear your ring for the rest of the summer, and come and kiss me goodnight every night after I'm in bed -"

"All right," Agony agreed hastily, with a sigh of resignation for this departure from her fixed principles regarding the lending of jewelry and about promiscuous demonstrations of affection, but peace in camp was worth the price.

Bengal claimed the ring at once, and then, after pawing Agony over like a bear cub, said a little shamefacedly, "I wish I were as good as you are. You're so honorable. How do you get such a 'nice sense of honor' as you have? I think I'd like to have one."

"Such a nice sense of honor as you have!" Agony jerked up as though she had been jabbed with a red hot needle. "Such a nice sense of honor as you have!" The words lingered in her ears like a mocking echo. The smile faded from her lips; her arm stiffened and dropped from Bengal's shoulder. The frank admiration in the younger girl's eyes cut her to the quick. With a haggard look she turned away from Bengal and wandered away to the other part of the island, away from the girls. Just now she could not bear to hear their gay, carefree voices. What would she not give, she thought to herself, to have nothing on her mind. She even envied rabbit-brained little Carmen Chadwick, who, if she had nothing in her head, had nothing on her conscience either.

"Who am I to talk of a 'nice sense of honor' to Bengal Virden?" she thought miserably. "I'm a whole lot worse than she. She's only a mischievous child, and doesn't know any better, but I do. I'm no better than Jane Pratt, either, even though I told Mrs. Grayson about her going out at night with boys from Camp Altamont." This matter of Jane Pratt had tormented Agony without ceasing. True to her contemptuous attitude toward Agony's plea that she break bonds no more, she had refused to tell Mrs. Grayson about her nocturnal canoe rides and thus had forced Agony to make good her threat and tell Mrs. Grayson herself. She had hoped and prayed that Jane would take the better course and confess her own wrong doing, but Jane did nothing of the kind, and there was only one course open to Agony. It was the rule of the camp that anyone seeing another breaking the rules must first give the offender the opportunity to confess, and if that failed must report the matter herself to the Doctor or Mrs. Grayson. So Agony was obliged to tell Mrs. Grayson that Jane was breaking the rules by slipping out nights and setting a bad example to the younger girls if any of them knew about it.

The matter caused more of a stir than Agony had expected,

and much more than she had wished for. Dr. Grayson prided himself upon the high standard of conduct which was maintained at his camp, and he knew that the mothers of his girls gave their daughters into his keeping with implicit faith that they would meet with no harmful influences while they were at Camp Keewaydin. If a rumor should ever get about that the girls from his camp went out in canoes after hours Keewaydin's reputation would suffer considerably. Dr. Grayson was outraged and thoroughly angry. He decided at once that Jane should be sent home in disgrace. That very day, however, Mrs. Grayson had received a letter saying that Jane's mother was quite ill in a sanatarium and that all upsetting news was being carefully kept away from her. She particularly desired that Jane should not come home, as there was no place for her to stay, and she was so much better taken care of in camp than she would be in a large city with no one to look after her. It was this letter that brought about a three-hour conference between the Doctor and Mrs. Grayson. Dr. Grayson was firm about sending Jane home in disgrace; Mrs. Grayson, filled with concern about her well loved friend, could not bear to risk upsetting her at this critical time by turning loose her unruly daughter. In the end Mrs. Grayson won her point, and Jane was allowed to stay in camp, but she was deprived of all canoe privileges for the remainder of the summer and forbidden to go on any of the trips with the camp. She was taken away from the easy-going, sound-sleeping councilor whose chaperonage she had succeeded in eluding and placed in a tent with Mrs. Grayson herself. Dr. Grayson called the whole camp together in council and explained the matter to the girls, dwelling upon the dishonorableness of breaking rules, and when he finished his talk there was small danger that even the smallest rule would be broken again during the summer. The sight of Jane Pratt called out in public to be censured was not one to be soon forgotten. Agony was commended by the Doctor for her firm stand in the matter, and praised because she did not take the easier course of remaining silent about it and running the risk of letting the reputation of the camp suffer.

Since then Jane, though somewhat subdued, had treated Agony with such marked animosity of manner that Agony hardly dared look at her. Added to her natural embarrassment at having been the in-former - a role which no one ever really enjoys - was the matter which lay like lead on Agony's own conscience and which tortured her out of all proportion to its real significance.

"Pretender!" the whole world seemed to shriek at her wherever she went.

Thus, although Agony apparently was throwing herself heart and soul into the preparations for Stunt Night, her mind was not on it half of the time and at times she was hardly conscious of the bustle and excitement around her.

These last three days the camp were as a house divided against itself, as far as the Avenue and the Alley were concerned. Such a gathering of groups into corners, such whispering and giggling, such sudden scattering at the approach of one from the other side! Sahwah spent two whole afternoons over on the far side of Whaleback, rehearsing her shipwreck, while the rest of the Alleyites worked up their parts on shore, trying to imitate the voices and characteristics of the various councilors. All went fairly well except the combination Tiny Armstrong. Carmen Chadwick, on top of Hinpoha, and draped up in Tiny's clothes, made a truly imposing figure that drew involuntary applause from the rest of the cast, but when Tiny spoke, the weak, piping voice that issued from the gigantic figure promptly threw them all into hysterics. The real Tiny's voice was as deep and resonant as a fog horn.

"That'll never do!" gasped Migwan through her tears of merriment. "That doesn't sound any more like Tiny than a chipping sparrow sounds like a lion. We'll have to get somebody with a deeper voice for the upper half of Tiny."

"But there isn't anybody else as light as Carmen," Hinpoha protested, "and I can't carry anybody that's any heavier."

Migwan wrinkled her brows and considered the matter.

"Oh, leave it the way it is," proposed Jo Severance. "They'll never notice a little thing like that."

"Yes, they will too," Gladys declared. "Anyway, you can't hear what Carmen says, and we want the folks to hear Tiny's speech, because it's so funny."

"But what are we going to do about it?" asked Migwan in perplexity.

"I know," said Katherine, rising to the occasion, as usual, "let the other half of Tiny do the talking. Hinpoha can make her voice quite deep and loud. It doesn't make any difference which half of Tiny talks, as long as the people hear it."

"Just the thing!" exclaimed Migwan delightedly. "Katherine, that head of yours will make your fortune yet. All right, Hinpoha, you speak Tiny's lines."

Hinpoha complied, and the effect of her voice coming apparently from beneath Tiny's ribs, while Tiny's mouth up above remained closed, was a great deal funnier than the first way.

"Never mind," said Migwan firmly, while the rest wept with laughter on each other's shoulders, "it sounds more like Tiny than the other way. You might stand with your back turned while you talk if Sinbad can't keep his face straight when he looks at you. You'd all better practice keeping your faces straight though. Katherine, you won't forget to get that gaudy blanket off the Lone Wolf's bed, will you?"

Migwan, her classic forehead streaked with perspiration and red color from the notebook in her hands, directed the rehearsal of her production all through the hot afternoon, until the lengthening shadows on the island warned them that is was time to get back to camp and prepare for the real performance.

The stunts were to begin at six-thirty, and would be held in the open space in front of Mateka, overlooking the river. The Avenue's stunt was to go on first, as the long end had fallen to them in the drawing of the cuts.

There was a great scurrying around after props after the Alleyites came back from the Island after that last rehearsal. Migwan, checking up her list, was constantly coming upon things that had been forgotten.

"Did somebody get Tiny Armstrong's red striped stockings?" she asked anxiously.

Nobody had remembered to get them. Katherine departed forthwith in quest of the necessary hosiery and found one of the stockings hanging out on the tent rope. The other was not in evidence. She was about to depart quietly without going into the tent, for one stocking was all that she needed, when a toothbrush suddenly whizzed past her ear, coming from the tent door. Laughing, she turned and went into the tent, first hastily concealing Tony's stocking in the front of her middy.

The flinger of the toothbrush turned out to be Tiny herself, who was sitting up in bed with her nightgown on.

"What's the matter, Tiny?" Katherine asked solicitously. "Are you sick? Aren't you going to get up to see the Stunts?"

"Get up!" shouted Tiny wrathfully. "I *can't* get up - I haven't any clothes."

"No clothes?" murmured Katherine in a puzzled tone.

"Everything's gone," continued Tiny plaintively, "bloomers, middies, shoes, stockings, hat, everything. Somebody has taken and hidden them for a joke, I suppose. I went to sleep here this afternoon, and when I woke up everything was gone."

Katherine suddenly grew very non-committal, although she

wanted to shriek with laughter. Oh-Pshaw, who had been sent after a suit of Tiny's that afternoon, had apparently made a pretty thorough job of it.

"Somebody must be playing a joke on you," Katherine remarked tranquilly, although she was conscious of the lump that Tiny's one remaining stocking made under her middy. "Never mind. Tiny, I'll go out and borrow some things for you to wear."

"But there's nothing of anybody's here that I can get into," mourned Tiny. "I'm four sizes bigger than the biggest of you. You'll have to find out who's hidden my things and bring them back."

Katherine was touched by Tiny's predicament, but the stunt had first claim on her. She came back presently with Tiny's bathing suit, which she had hanging on a nearby tree, and a long raincoat of Dr. Grayson's, together with his tennis shoes. She even had to beg a pair of his socks from Mrs. Grayson, for all of Tiny's that had not been borrowed were away at the laundry. And in that collection of clothes Tiny had to go and sit in the Judges' box at the Stunts, but her good nature was not ruffled one whit on account of it.

Katherine was still getting Tiny into her improvised wardrobe when a loud hubbub proclaimed the arrival of the boys from Camp Altamont, and at the same time the bugle sounded the assembly call for the girls. The Alleyites, bursting with impatience for the time of their own stunt to arrive, settled themselves in their places to watch the Avenue stunt. The bugle sounded again, and the chairman of the Avenue stunt stood up.

"Our stunt tonight," she announced, "tells a hitherto unpublished one of Gulliver's Travels, namely, his voyage to the Land of the Keewaydins."

The Alley sat up with one convulsive jerk. "Gulliver's Travels!"

That sounded nearly like their own idea.

Then the stunt proceeded, beginning with Gulliver wrecked on the shore of the Land of the Keewaydins. Undine Girelle was Gulliver, and her shipwreck was trully a thrilling one. She finally landed, spent with swimming, on the shore, and was taken in hand by the friendly Keewaydins, who proceeded to show him their customs. The Alley gradually turned to stone as they saw practically the very same things they were planning to do, being performed before their eyes by the Avenue. There was Miss Peckham and the stocking-snake (that explained to Katherine why she had only been able to find one of Tiny's red and black stockings); there was Tiny herself, and made out of two girls, just as they were going to do it! There was Dr. Grayson, there were all the other councilors; there was a burlesque on camp life almost exactly as they had planned to do it!

The boys and the councilors applauded wildly, but the Alleyites, too surprised and taken back to be appreciative, merely looked at each other in mute consternation.

"Somebody gave away our secret!" was the first indignant thought that flashed into the minds of the Alleyites, but the utter astonishment of the Avenue when the Alley said that their stunt was practically the same, soon convinced them that the whole thing was a mere co-incidence.

"It's a wonder I didn't suspect anything when I found that all of Tiny's clothes were gone," said Katherine. "That should have told me that someone else was impersonating her."

The Alley at first declined to put on their stunt, since it was so nearly the same as the other, but the audience refused to let them off, insisting that they had come to see two stunts, and they were going to see two, even if they *were* alike.

"We can still judge which is the best," said Dr. Grayson. "In fact, it is an unusual opportunity. Usually the stunts are so different that it is hard to tell which is the better, but having two performances on the same subject gives a rare chance to consider the fine points."

So the Alley went ahead with their stunt just as if nothing out of the way had occurred, and the judges applauded them just as wildly as they had the others. In the end, the honors had to be evenly divided between the two, for the judges declared that one was just as good as the other and it was impossible to decide between them.

"And we were so dead sure that the Avenue would never be able to think up anything nearly as clever as ours," remarked Sahwah ruefully, as she prepared for bed that night.

"I'm beginning to come to the conclusion," replied Hinpoha with a sleepy yawn, "that it isn't safe to be too sure of anything. You never can tell from the outside of people what they are likely to have inside of them."

"No, you can't" echoed Agony soberly.

CHAPTER XIII

THEIR NATIVE WILDS

Miss Judy's hat was more or less a barometer of the state of her emotions. Worn far back on her head with its brim turned up, it indicated that she was at peace with all the world and upon pleasure bent; tipped over one ear, it denoted intense preoccupation with business affairs; pulled low over her eyes, it was a sign of extreme vexation. This morning the hat was pulled so far down over her face that only the tip of her chin was visible. Katherine, stopping to help her run a canoe up on the bank after swimming hour, noticed the unnecessary vehemence of her movements, and asked mildly as to the cause.

Miss Judy replied with a single explosive exclamation of "Monty!"

"Monty!" Katherine echoed inquringly. "What's that?"

"You're right, it *is* a 'what'," replied Miss Judy emphatically, "although it usually goes down in the catalog as a 'who.' It's my cousin, Egmont Satter-white," she continued in explanation. "He's coming to pay us a visit at camp."

"Yes," said Katherine. "What is he like?"

"Like?" repeated Miss Judy derisively. "He's like the cock who thought the sun didn't get up until he crowed - so conceited;

only he goes still farther. He doesn't see what need there is for the sun at all while he is there to shed his light. He's the only child of his adoring mother, and she's cultivated him like a rare floral specimen; private tutors and all that sort of thing. Now he's learned everything there is to know, and he's ready to write a book. He regards his fellow creatures as quaint and curious specimens, 'rather diverting for one to observe, don't you know,' but not at all important. I suppose he's going to put a chapter in his book about girls, because he wrote to father and announced that he was going to run up for a week or so and observe us in our native wilds - that was the delicate way he put it. He'll probably set down everything he sees in a notebook and then go home and solemnly write his chapter, wise as Solomon."

"What a bore!" sighed Katherine. "I hate to be stared at, and 'observed' for somebody else's benefit."

"Monty's a pest!" Miss Judy exploded wrathfully. "I don't see why father ever told him he could come. He's under no obligations to him - we're only third cousins, and Monty considers us far, far beneath him at best. But you know how father is - hospitality with a capital H. So we're doomed to a visitation from Monty."

"When is he coming?" asked Katherine, smiling at Miss Judy's lugubrious tone.

"The day after tomorrow," replied Miss Judy. "The Thursday afternoon boat has the honor of bringing him."

"'O better that her shattered hulk should sink beneath the wave,' eh?" remarked Katherine sympathetically.

"Katherine," said Miss Judy feelingly, "*vous et moi* we speak the same language, *n'est-ce pas?*"

"We do," agreed Katherine laughingly.

That evening when all the campers were gathered around the fire in the bungalow, listening to Dr. Grayson reading "The Crock of Gold" to the pattering accompaniment of the raindrops on the roof, Miss Judy went into the camp office to answer the telephone, and came out with a look of half-humorous exasperation on her face.

"What is it?" asked Dr. Grayson, pausing in his reading.

"It's Cousin Monty," announced Miss Judy. He's at Emmet's Landing, two stops down the river. He decided to come to camp a day earlier than he had written. He got off the boat at Emmet's Landing to sketch an 'exquisite' bit of scenery that he spied there. Now he's marooned at Emmet's Landing and can't get a boat to bring him to camp. He decided to stay there all night, and found a room, but the bed didn't look comfortable. He wants us to come and get him."

"At this time of night!" Dr. Grayson exclaimed involuntarily. He recovered himself instantly. "Ah yes, certainly, of course. I'll go and get him. Tell him I'll come for him."

"But it's raining pitchforks," demurred Miss Judy.

"Ah well, never mind, I'll go anyhow," said her father composedly.

"I'll go with you," declared Miss Judy firmly. "I'll run the launch." As she passed by Katherine on her way out of the bungalow she flashed her a meaning look, which Katherine answered with a sympathetic grimace.

In the morning when camp assembled for breakfast there was Cousin Egmont sitting beside Dr. Grayson at the table, notebook in hand, looking about him in a loftily curious way. He was a small, slightly built youth, sallow of complexion and insignificant of feature, with pale hair brushed up into an exaggerated pompadour, and a neat little moustache. In contrast to Dr. Grayson's heroic proportions he looked like a

Vest Pocket Edition alongside of an Unabridged.

"Nice little camp you have here, Uncle, very," he drawled, peering languidly through his huge spectacles at the shining river and the far off rolling hills beyond. "Nothing like the camps I've seen in Switzerland, though. For real camps you want to go to Switzerland, Uncle. A chap I know goes there every summer. Of course, for a girl's camp this does very well, very. Pretty fair looking lot of girls you have, Uncle. All from picked families, eh? Require references and all that sort of thing?"

Dr. Grayson made a deprecatory gesture with his hand and looked uneasily around the table, to see if Egmont's remarks were being overheard. But Mrs. Grayson sat on the other side of Egmont, and the seat next to the Doctor was vacant, so there was really no one within hearing distance except the Lone Wolf, who sat opposite to Mrs. Grayson, and she was deeply engrossed in conversation with the girl on the other side of her.

Monty prattled on. "You see, Uncle, I wouldn't have come up here to observe if I thought they were not from the best families. Anybody I'd care to write about - you understand, Uncle."

"Yes, I understand," replied Dr. Grayson quizzically. "Have you taken any notes yet?" he continued.

"Nothing yet," Monty admitted, "but I mean to begin immediately after breakfast. I mean to flit unobtrusively about Camp, Uncle, and watch the young ladies when they do not suspect I am around, taking down their innocent girlish conversation among themselves. So much more natural that way, Uncle, very!"

Dr. Grayson hurriedly took a huge mouthful of water, and then choked on it in a very natural manner, and Miss Judy's coming in with the mail bag at that moment caused a welcome diversion.

"Ah, good morning, Cousin Judith," drawled Monty. "I see you didn't get up as early as the rest of us. Perhaps the fatigue of last night -"

"I've been down the river for the mail," replied Miss Judy shortly. Then she turned her back on him and spoke to her father. "The weather is settled for this week. That rainstorm last night cleared things up beautifully. We ought to take the canoe trip, the one up to the Falls."

"That's so," agreed Dr. Grayson. "How soon can you arrange to go?"

"Tomorrow," replied Miss Judy.

"Ah, a canoe trip," cried Monty brightly. "I ought to get quantities of notes from that."

Miss Judy eyed him for a moment with an unfathomable expression on her face, then turned away and began to talk to the Lone Wolf.

All during Morning Sing Monty sat in a corner and took notes with a silver pencil in an embossed leather notebook, staring now at this girl, now at that, until she turned fiery red and fidgeted. After Morning Sing he established himself on a rocky ledge just below Bedlam, where, hidden by the bushes, he sat ready to take down the innocent conversation of the young ladies among themselves as they made their tents ready for tent inspection.

Katherine and Oh-Pshaw were in the midst of tidying up when the Lone Wolf dropped in to return a flashlight she had borrowed the night before. She strolled over to the railing at the back of the tent and peered over it. A gleam came into her eye as she noticed that one of the bushes just below the tent on the slope toward the river was waving slightly in an opposite direction from the way in which the wind was blowing. Stepping back into the tent she stopped beside Bedlam's water pail, newly filled for tent inspection.

"Your water looks sort of - er - muddy," she remarked artfully. "Hadn't you better throw it out and get some fresh? Here, I'll do it for you. I'm not busy."

She picked up the brimming pail and emptied it over the back railing, right over the spot where she had seen the bush waving. Immediately there came a curious sound out of the bush - half gasp and half yell, and out sprang Monty, dripping like a rat, and fled down the path toward the bungalow, without ever looking around.

"Why, he was down there *listening*," Katherine exclaimed in disgust. "Oh, how funny it was," she remarked to the Lone Wolf, "that you happened to come in and dump that pail of water over the railing just at that time."

"It certainty was," the Lone Wolf acquiesced gravely, as she departed with the pail in the direction of the spring.

Cousin Monty flitted unobtrusively to his tent, got on dry garments, fished another notebook out of his bag, and set out once more in quest of local color. He wandered down to Mateka, where Craft Hour was in progress. A pottery craze had struck camp, and the long tables were filled with girls rolling and patting lumps of plastic clay into vases, jars, bowls, plates and other vessels. Cousin Monty strolled up and down, contemplating the really creditable creation of the girls with a condescending patronage that made them feel like small children in the kindergarten. He gave the art director numerous directions as to how she might improve her method of teaching, and benevolently pointed out to a number of the girls how the things they were making were all wrong.

Finally he came and stood by Hinpoha, who was putting the finishing touches on the decoration of a rose jar, an exquisite thing, with a raised design in rose petals. Hinpoha was smoothing out the flat background of her design when Monty paused beside her.

"You're not holding your instrument right." he remarked patronizingly. "Let me show you how." He took the instrument from Hinpoha's unwilling hand, and turning it wrong way up, proceeded to scrape back and forth. At the third stroke it went too far, and gouged out a deep scratch right through the design, clear across the whole side of the vase.

"Ah, a little scratch," he remarked airily. "Ah, sorry, really, very. But it can soon be remedied. A little dob of clay, now."

"Let me fix it myself," said Hinpoha firmly, with difficulty keeping her exasperation under the surface, and without more ado seized her mutilated treasure from his hands.

"Ah, yes, of course," murmured Monty, and wandered on to the next table.

By the time the day was over Cousin Monty was about as popular as a hornet. "How long is he going to stay?" the girls asked each other in comical dismay. "A week? Oh, my gracious, how can we ever stand him around here a week?"

"Is he going along with us on the canoe trip?" Katherine asked Miss Judy as she helped her check over supplies for the expedition.

"He is that," replied Miss Judy. "He's going along to pester us just as he has been doing - probably worse, because he's had a night to think up a whole lot more fool questions to ask than he could think of yesterday."

And it was even so. Monty, notebook in hand, insisted upon knowing the why and wherefore of every move each one of the girls made until they began to flee at his approach. "Why are you tying up your ponchos that way? That isn't the way. Now if you will just let me show you -"

"Why you are putting that stout girl" - indicating Bengal - "in the stern of the canoe? You want the weight up front - that's the newest way."

"Now Uncle, just let me show you a trick or two about stowing away those supplies. You're not in the least scientific about it."

Thus he buzzed about, inquisitive and officious.

Katherine and Miss Judy looked into each other's eyes and exchanged exasperated glances. Then Katherine's eye took on a peculiar expression, the one which always registered the birth of an idea. At dinner, which came just before the expedition started, she was late - a good twenty minutes. She tranquilly ate what was left for her and was extremely polite to Counsin Monty, answering his continuous questions about the coming trip with great amiability, even enthusiasm. Miss Judy looked at her curiously.

The expedition started. Monty, who had Miss Peckham in the canoe with him - she being the only one who would ride with him - insisted upon going at the head of the procession. "I'll paddle so much faster than the rest of you," he said airily, "that I'll want room to go ahead. I don't want to be held back by the rest of you when I shall want to put on a slight spurt now and then. That is the way I like to go, now fast, now slowly, as inclination dictates, without having to keep my pace down to that of others. I will start first, Uncle, and lead the line."

"All right," replied Dr. Grayson a trifle wearily. "You may lead the line."

The various canoes had been assigned before, so there was no confusion in starting. The smallest of the canoes had been given to Monty because there would be only two in it. Conscious that he was decidedly ornamental in his speckless white flannels and silk shirt he helped Miss Peckham into the boat with exaggerated gallantry, all the while watching out of the corner of his eye to see if Pom-pom was looking at him. He had been trying desperately to flirt with her ever since his arrival, and had begged her to go with him in the canoe on the trip, all in vain. Nevertheless, he was still buzzing around her and playing to the audience of her eyes. By fair means or foul he meant to get the privilege of having her with him on the return trip. Miss Peckham, newly graduated into the canoe privilege, was nervous and fussy, and handled her paddle as gingerly as if it were a gun.

"Ah, let me do all the paddling," he insisted, knowing that Pom-pom, in a nearby canoe, could hear him. "I could not think of allowing you to exert yourself. It is the man's place, you know. You really mustn't think of it."

Miss Peckham laid down her paddle with a sigh of relief, and Monty, with a graceful gesture, untied the canoe and pushed it out from the dock. Behind him the line of boats were all waiting to start.

"Here we go!" he shouted loudly, as he dipped his paddle. In a moment all the canoes were in motion. Monty, at the head, seemed to find the paddling more difficult than he had expected. He dipped his paddle with great vigor and vim, but the canoe only went forward a few inches at each stroke. One by one the canoes began to pass him, their occupants casting amusing glances at him as he perspired over his paddle. He redoubled his efforts, he strained every sinew, and the canoe did go a little faster, but not nearly as fast as the others were going.

"What's the matter, Monty, is your load too heavy for you?" called out Miss Judy.

"Not at all," replied Monty doggedly. "I'm a little out of form, I guess. This arm - I strained it last spring - seems to have gone lame all of a sudden."

"Would you like to get in a canoe with some of the girls?" asked Dr. Grayson solicitously.

"I would *not*," replied Monty somewhat peevishly. "Please let me alone, Uncle, I'll be all right in a minute. Don't any of you bother about me, I'll follow you at my leisure. When I get used to paddling again I'll very soon overtake you even if you have a good start."

The rest of the canoes swept by, and Monty and Miss Peckham soon found themselves alone on the river.

"Hadn't I better help you paddle?" asked Miss Peckham anxiously. She was beginning to distrust the powers of her ferryman.

"No, no, no," insisted Monty, stung to the quick by the concern in her voice. "I can do it very well alone, I tell you."

He kept at it doggedly for another half hour, stubbornly refusing to accept any help, until the canoe came *to* a dead stop. No amount of paddling would budge it an inch; it was apparently anchored. Puzzled, Monty peered into the river to find the cause of the stoppage. The water was deep, but there were many snags and obstructions under the surface. Something was holding him, that was plain, but what it was he could not find out, nor could he get loose from it. The water was too deep to wade ashore, and there was nothing to do but sit there and try to get loose by means of the paddle, a proceeding which soon proved fruitless. In some mysterious way they were anchored out in mid stream at a lonely place in the river where no one would be likely to see them for a long time. The others were out of sight long ago, having obeyed Monty's injunction to let him alone.

Monty, in his usual airy way, tried to make the best of the situation and draw attention away from his evident inability to cope with the situation. "Ah, pleasant it is to sit out here and bask in the warm sunshine," he murmured in dulcet tones.

"The view is exquisite here, *n'est-ce pas*? I could sit here all day and look at that mountain in the distance. It reminds me somewhat of the Alps, don't you know."

Miss Peckham gazed unhappily at the mountain, which was merely a blur in the distance. "Do you think we'll have to sit here all night?" she asked anxiously.

Monty exerted himself to divert her. "How does it come that I have never met you before, Miss Peckham? Really, I didn't know that Uncle Clement had such delightful relations. Can it be that you are really his cousin? It hardly seems possible that you are old enough. Sitting there with the breeze toying with you hair that way you look like a young girl, no older than Judith herself."

Now this was quite a large dose to swallow, but Miss Peckham swallowed it, and much delighted with the gallant youth, so much more appreciative of her than the others at camp, she sat listening attentively to his prattle of what he had seen and done, keeping her hat off the while to let her hair ripple in the breeze the way he said he liked it, regardless of the fact that the sun was rather hot.

In something over an hour a pair of rowboats came along filled with youngsters who thought it great sport to rescue the pair in the marooned canoe, and who promptly discovered the cause of the trouble. It was an iron kettle full of stones, fastened to the bottom of the canoe with a long wire, which had wedged itself in among the branches of a submerged tree in the river and anchored the canoe firmly.

"Somebody's played a trick on us!" exclaimed Miss Peckham wrathfully. "Somebody at camp deliberately fastened that kettle of stones to the bottom of the canoe to make it hard for you to paddle. That's just what you might have expected from those girls. They're playing tricks all the time. They have no respect for anyone."

Monty turned a dull red when he saw that kettle full of stones, and he, too, sputtered with indignation. "Low brow trick," he exclaimed loftily, but he felt quite the reverse of lofty. "This must be Cousin Judith's doing," he continued angrily, remembering the subtle antagonism that had sprung up between his cousin and himself.

His dignity was too much hurt to allow him to follow the rest of the party now. Disgusted, he turned back in the direction of camp. By the time he arrived he began to feel that he did not want to stay long enough to see the enjoyment of his cousin over his discomfiture. He announced his intention of leaving that very night, paddling down the river to the next landing, and boarding the evening boat.

Miss Peckham suddenly made up her mind, too. "I'm going with you." She declared. "I'm not going to stay here and be insulted any longer. It'll serve them right to do without my services as councilor for the rest of the summer. I'll just leave a note for Mrs. Grayson and slip out quietly with you."

When the expedition returned the following day both Pecky and Monty were gone.

Bengal raised such a shout of joy when she heard of the departure of her despised councilor that her tent mates were obliged to restrain her transports for the look of the thing, but they, too, were somewhat relieved to be rid of her.

The reason of the double departure remained a mystery in camp until the very end, but there were a select few that always winked solemnly at one another whenever Dr. Grayson wondered what had become of his largest camping kettle.

CHAPTER XIV

REGATTA DAY

The long anticipated, the much practiced for Regatta Day had dawned, bringing with it crowds of visitors to Camp. It was Camp Keewaydin's great day, when the Avenue and the Alley struggled for supremacy in aquatics. The program consisted of contests in swimming and diving, canoe upsetting and righting, demonstrations of rescue work, stunts and small canoe races, and ended up with a race between the two war canoes. Visitors came from all the summer resorts around, and many of the girls' parents and friends came to see their daughters perform.

The dock and the diving platform were gay with flags; the tents had been tidied up to wax-like neatness and decorated with wild flowers until they looked like so many royal bowers; in Mateka an exhibition of Craft Work was laid out on the long tables - pottery and silver work and weaving and decorating. Hinpoha's rose jar, done with infinite pains and patience after its unfortunate meeting with Cousin Egmont, held the place of honor in the centre of the pottery table, and her silver candlesticks, done in an exquisite design of dogwood blossoms, was the most conspicuous piece on the jewelry table.

"Hinpoha'll get the Craft Work prize, without any doubt," said Migwan to Agony as they stood helping to arrange the articles in the Craft Work exhibit. "She's a real artist. The rest of us are just dabblers. It's queer, though, I admire that little plain pottery bowl I made myself more than I do Hinpoha's wonderful rose jar. I suppose it's because I made it all myself, it's like my own child. There's a thrill about doing things yourself that makes you hold your head higher even if other people don't think it's anything very wonderful. Don't you feel that way, Agony?"

"I suppose so," murmured Agony, rather absently, her animation falling away from her in an instant, and a weary look creeping into her eyes.

"That's the way you must feel all the time since you did that splendid thing," continued Migwan warmly. "No matter where you are, or how hard a thing you're up against, you have only to think, 'I was equal to a great emergency once; I did the brave and splendid thing when the time came,' and then you'll be equal to it again. O, how wonderful it must be to know that when the time comes you won't be a coward! O Agony, we're all so proud of you!" cried Migwan, interrupting herself to give Agony an adoring hug. "All the Winnebagos will be braver and better because you did that, Agony. They'll be ashamed to be any less than you are."

"It wasn't anything much that - I did," Agony protested in a flat voice.

Migwan, busy straightening out the rows of bracelets and rings, did not notice the hunted expression in Agony's face, and soon the bugle sounded, calling all the girls together on the dock.

Only those who have ever taken part in Regatta Day will get the real thrill when reading an account of it in cold print - the thrill which comes from seeing dozens of motor boats filled with spectators lined up on the river, and crowds standing on the shore; the sun shining in dazzling splendor on the ripples; the flags snapping in the breeze, the starters with their pistols standing out on the end of the dock, the canoes rocking alongside, straining at their ropes as if impatient to be off in the races; the crews, in their new uniforms, standing nervously around their captains, getting their last instructions and examining their paddles for any possible cracks; the councilors rushing around preparing the props for the stunts they were directing; and over all a universal atmosphere of suspense, of tenseness, of excitement.

The Alleys wore bright red bathing caps, the Avenues blue; otherwise they wore the regulation Camp bathing suits, all alike. First on the program came the demonstrations - canoe tipping, rescuing a drowning person, resuscitation. Sahwah won the canoe tipping contest, getting her canoe righted in one minute less time than it took Undine Girelle, so the first score went to the Alley. The Avenue had a speedy revenge, however, for Undine took first honors in the diving exhibition which followed immediately after. Even the Winnebagos, disappointed as they were that Sahwah had not won out, admitted that Undine's performance was unequalled, and joined heartily in the cheers that greeted the announcement of her winning. In the smaller contests the Avenue and the Alley were pretty well matched, and at the end of the swimming and small canoe races the score was tied between them. This left the war canoe race, which counted ten points, to decide the championship.

A round of applause greeted the two crews as they marched out on the dock to the music of the Camp band and took their places in the war canoes. Sahwah was Captain of the Dolphins, the Alley crew; Undine commanded the Avenue Turtles. Agony was stern paddler of the Dolphin, the most important position next to the Captain. Prominence had come to her in many ways since she had become the camp heroine; positions of trust and honor fell to her thick and fast without her making any special efforts to get them. If nothing succeeds like success it is equally true that nothing brings honor like honor already achieved. To her who hath shall be given.

Besides Sahwah and Agony the Dolphin crew consisted of Hinpoha, Migwan, Gladys, Katherine, Jo Severance, Jean

Hildegard G. Frey

Lawrence, Bengal Virden, Oh-Pshaw, and two girls from Aloha, Edith Anderson and Jerry Mortimer, a crew picked after severe tests which eliminated all but the most expert paddlers. That the Winnebagos had all passed the test was a matter of considerable pride to them, and also to Nyoda, to whom they had promptly written the good news.

"I am not surprised, though," she had written in return. "I am never surprised at anything my girls accomplish. I always expect you to do things - and you do them."

Quickly the two Captains brought their canoes out to the starting line and sat waiting for the shot from the starter's pistol. The command "Paddles Up!" had been given, and twenty-four broad yellow blades were poised stiffly in air, ready for the plunge into the shining water below. A hush fell upon the watching crowd; the silence was so intense that the song of a bird on the roof of Mateka could be plainly heard. A smile came to Sahwah's lips as she heard the joyous thrill of the bird. An omen of victory, she said to herself.

Then the pistol cracked. Almost simultaneously with its report came her clear command, "Down paddles!" Twelve paddles dipped as one and the Dolphin shot forward a good five feet on the very first stroke. The race was on.

The course was from the dock to Whaleback Island, around the Island and back to the starting point.

Until the Island was reached the canoes kept practically abreast, now one forging a few inches ahead, now the other, but always evening up the difference before long. As the pull toward Whaleback was downstream both crews made magnificent speed with apparently little effort. The real struggle lay in rounding the Island and making the return pull upstream. The Dolphin had the inside track, a fact which at first caused her crew to exult, because of the shorter turn, but they soon found that the advantage gained in this way was practically offset by the force of the current close to the Island, which made it difficult for the boat to keep in her course. It took all of Agony's skill as stern paddler to swing the Dolphin around and keep her out of the current. The two canoes were still abreast when they recovered from the turn and started back upstream. As they rounded the large pile of rocks which formed a bodyguard around Whaleback, the current caught the Dolphin and gave her a half turn back toward the Island. Agony bore quickly down on her paddle to offset the pull of the current; it struck an unexpected rock underneath the surface and twisted itself out of her hands. In a moment the current had caught it and whirled it out of reach. Only an instant did Agony waste looking after it in consternation.

"Give me your paddle," she said quickly to Bengal Virden, who sat in front of her, and took it out of her hand without ceremony.

The Dolphin righted herself without any further trouble and came out into the straight upstream course only a little behind the Turtle. Then the real race began.

In a few moments the Turtle had forged ahead, and it soon became apparent that the Dolphin, carrying one member of the crew who was not paddling, could not hope to keep up.

"Bengal," megaphoned Sahwah, taking in the situation at a glance, "you'll have to get out. You're dead weight. Jump and swim back to the island. The water isn't deep here."

Bengal refused. "I want to stay in the race."

Sahwah gave a disgusted snort into the megaphone. Agony cast herself into the breach and made use of Bengal's crush on her for the sake of the Alley cause. "If you do it, Bengal, I'll come and sleep with you all the rest of the time we're in camp."

Bengal rose to the bait. "I'll do it for you," she said adoringly, and promptly jumped out of the canoe and swam back the short distance to the Island where she was soon picked up by one of the visiting launches and carried to the sidelines.

Relieved of Bengal's weight, which had been considerable, the Dolphin quickly recovered herself and caught up with the Turtle; then slowly worked into the lead. She did not lose the lead again, but came under the line a good three feet ahead of the Turtle. The long anticipated struggle was over and the Alley was the victor.

The rest of the Alley rushed down upon the dock and dragged the victorious crew up out of the Dolphin as she came up alongside of the dock, and lifting them to their shoulders carried them to shore in a triumphal procession, with waving banners, and ear splitting cheers, and songs which excess of emotion rendered slightly off key. Bengal was brought over and given a separate ovation for having so nobly sacrificed herself for the cause of the Alley; Agony also came in for a great deal of extra cheering because she had acted so promptly when she lost her paddle, and Sahwah - well, Sahwah was the Captain, and when did the Captain of a victorious crew ever suffer neglect from the side he represented?

Until Taps sounded that night the Alley celebrated its victory, and the last thing they did for joy was to carry all the beds out of the tents and set them in one long row in the Alley, and when Miss Judy went the last rounds there they lay, all linked together arm in arm, smiling one long smile which reached from one end of the Alley to the other.

CHAPTER XV

THE BUFFALO ROBE

"Sunset and evening star,
And one clear call for me!"

The familiar lines slipped softly from Miss Amesbury's lips as
she leaned luxuriously against the canoe cushions, watching
the vivid glows of the sunset. It was the hour after supper,
when the Camp girls were free to do as they pleased, and
Agony and Miss Amesbury had come out for a quiet paddle on
the river. The excitement of Regatta Day had subsided, and
Camp was jogging peacefully toward its close. Only a few
more days and then the *Carribou* would come and take away
the merry, frolicking campers, and the Alley and the Avenue
alike would know desolation.

All over there were signs that told summer was drawing to a
close. The fields were gay with goldenrod and wild asters, the
swamp maples had begun to flame in the woods, and there was
a crisp tang in the air that sent the blood racing in the veins
like a draught of strong, new wine. All these things, as well as
the westward shifting of the summer constellations, which a
month before had reigned supreme on the meridian, told that
the summer was drawing to an end.

Never had the friends at Camp seemed so jolly and dear as in
this last week when the days together were numbered, and
every sunrise brought them one degree nearer the parting.

Hildegard G. Frey

Everyone was filled with the desire to make the most of these last few days; there was a frantic scramble to do the things that had been talked of all summer, but which had been crowded out by other things, and especially there was a busy taking of pictures of favorite councilors and best friends. Pom-pom, Miss Judy, Tiny Armstrong and the Lone Wolf could be seen at almost any hour of the day "looking pleasant" while some girl snapped their pictures.

"If anyone else asks me to pose for a picture today I shall explode!" declared Tiny Armstrong at last. "I've stood in the sun until I'm burned to a cinder, and I've 'looked pleasant' until my face aches. I'm going on a strike!"

Agony found herself possessed in these last days of an ever increasing desire to be with Miss Amesbury, to hear her talk and watch the expressions play over her beautiful, mobile face. For this brilliant and accomplished woman Agony had conceived an admiration which stirred the very depths of her intense, passionate nature. To be famous and fascinating like Miss Amesbury, this was the secret ambition that filled her restless soul. To be near her now, to have her all to herself in a canoe in this most beautiful hour of the day, thrilled Agony to the verge of intoxication. Her voice trembled when she spoke, her hand shook as she dipped the paddle.

The wide flaming fire of the sunset toned down to a tawny orange; then faded into a pale primrose; the big, bright evening star appeared in the west. From all the woods around came the goodnight twitter of the birds.

"Sunset and evening star -" repeated Agony softly, echoing the words Miss Amesbury had spoken a few moments before. "Oh," she declared, "sunset is the most perfect time of the day for me. I feel just bewitched. I could do anything just at sunset; all my dreams seem about to come true."

And drifting there in the rosy afterglow they talked of dreams and hopes, and ambitions, and Agony laid her soul bare to the older woman. She spoke of the things she planned to do, the career of social service she had laid out for herself, and of the influence for good she would be in the world - all of this to take place in the golden sometime when she would be grown up and out of school.

Miss Amesbury heard her through with a quiet smile. Agony looked up, encountered her gaze and stopped speaking. "Don't you think I can?" she asked quickly.

"It is possible," replied Miss Amesbury tranquilly. "Everything is possible. 'We are all architects of fate;' you must have heard that line quoted before. Everyone carries his future in his own hands; fate has really nothing to do with it. Whatever kind of bud we are, such a flower we will be. We cannot make ourselves; all we can do is blossom. This Other Person that you see in your golden dreams is after all only you, changed from the You that you are now into the You that you hope to be. If we are little, stunted buds we cannot be big, glorious blossoms. The Future is only a great many Nows added up. It is the things you are doing now that will make your future glorious or abject. To be a noble woman you must have been a noble girl. You are setting your face now in the direction in which you are going to travel. Every worthy action you perform now will open the way for more worthy actions in the future, and the same is true of unworthy ones."

Agony sat very still.

"It is the thing we stand for ourselves that makes us an influence for evil or good," continued Miss Amesbury, "not the thing that we preach. That is why so much of the so-called 'uplift work' in the world has no effect upon the persons we are trying to uplift - we try to give them something which we do not possess ourselves. We cannot give something which we don't possess, don't ever forget that, dear child. Be sure that your own torch is burning brightly before you attempt to light someone else's with it.

Hildegard G. Frey

"You know, Agony, that after Jesus went away out of the Temple at the age of twelve years we do not hear of him again until he was a grown man of thirty. What took place in those years we will never know exactly; but in those Silent Years He prepared Himself for His glorious destiny. He must have conquered Self, day by day, until He was master over all his moods and desires, to be able to influence others so profoundly. He must have developed a sympathetic understanding of His friends and playfellows, to know so intimately the troubles of all the multitudes which he afterwards met. These are *your* Silent Years, Agony. What you make of them will determine your future."

*   *   *   *   *

"Why, where is everybody?" Agony asked wonderingly as they drew their canoe up on the dock and went up the hill path. Nobody was in sight, but a subdued sound of cheering and laughter came from the direction of Mateka.

"Oh, I forgot," cried Agony. "There *is* something tonight in Mateka, a meeting. Dr. Grayson announced it this noon at dinner, but I forgot all about it and hurried through supper tonight so I could come out on the river with you. I wonder what it was about. Come on, let's go up, maybe we can get there before it's over."

They were just going up the steps of Mateka when half a dozen girls rushed out of the door and fell upon Agony.

"Where on earth have you been? We've been hunting all over camp for you. You're elected most popular camper! You've won the Buffalo Robe! Oh, Agony, you've won the Buffalo Robe!"

It was Oh-Pshaw who was speaking, and she cast herself on her twin's neck and kissed her rapturously.

Agony stood very still on the steps, looking in a dazed sort of way from one to the other of the faces around her.

"Oh, Agony, don't you understand? You've won the Buffalo Robe!" Oh-Pshaw repeated laughingly. "We had the election tonight. You won by a big majority. It's all on account of the robin. Nobody else had done anything nearly so splendid. Oh, but I'm proud to be your twin sister!"

Then all the rest came out of Mateka and surrounded Agony, telling her how glad they were she had won the Buffalo Robe, and they ended up by taking her on their shoulders into Mateka and setting her down before the Robe where it hung on the wall. It would be formally presented to her at the farewell banquet two nights later.

"We're going to paint a robin on it as a record of your brave deed," said Migwan. "Hinpoha is working on the design right now."

Agony's emotions were tumultous as she stood there in Mateka before the Buffalo Robe with the girls singing cheer after cheer to her. First triumph flooded her whole being, and delight and satisfaction that she had won the biggest honor in Camp took complete possession of her. The most popular girl in camp! The desire of her heart, born on that first, far off day at camp, had been realized. The precious trophy was hers to take home, to exhibit to Nyoda. She was the center of all eyes; her name was on every lip.

Then, in the midst of her triumph the leaden weight began to press down on her spirits, pulling her back to realization. Her smile faded, her lips trembled, her voice was so husky that she could hardly speak.

"It's - so - hot - in - here," she panted. "Let me go out where it's cool."

And all unsuspecting they led her out and bore her to her tent in triumph.

CHAPTER XVI

THE TORCH KINDLES

Even the Winnebagos wondered slightly at the extremely quiet way in which Agony received the great honor that had been bestowed upon her. She did not expand as usual under the influence of the limelight until she fairly radiated light. She hummed no gay songs, she played no pranks on her friends; she did not outdo herself in work and play as she used to in the days of yore when she was the observed of all observers. Silent and pensive she wandered about Camp the next day and seemed rather to be shunning the gay groups in Mateka and on the beach. Most of the girls believed that Agony's silence proceeded from the genuine humility of the truly great when singled out for honor, and admired her all the more for her sober, pensive air. She found herself overwhelmed with requests to stand for her picture, and the younger girls thronged her tent, begging for locks of hair to take home as keepsakes. Agony escaped from them as best she could without offending them.

She sedulously avoided Mateka, for there sat Hinpoha busily painting robins on the place cards for the banquet which was to take place the following night. This banquet was given each year as a wind-up to the camp activities, with the winner of the Buffalo Robe in the place of honor at the head of the table. Agony felt weak every time she thought of that banquet. Why had she not the courage to confess the deception to Dr. Grayson, and give up the Buffalo Robe, she thought miserably.

No, she could never do that. The terrific pride which was Agony's very life and soul would not let her humble herself. The pain it would give Dr. Grayson, the astonishment and disappointment of the Winnebagos, the coldness of the beloved councilors - and Jane Pratt! How could she ever humble herself before Jane Pratt and witness Jane's keen relish of her downfall? She could hear Jane's spiteful laughter, her malicious remarks, her unrestrained rejoicing over the situation.

And Miss Amesbury! No, she could never let Miss Amesbury know what a cheat she was. No, no, the thing had gone too far, she must see it through now. Better to endure the gnawings of conscience than give herself away now. And Nyoda - Nyoda who had praised her so sincerely, and Slim and the Captain, who thought it was a "bully stunt" - could she let them know that it was all a lie? She shrank back shuddering from the notion. No, she must go on. No one would ever find it out now. Other people had received honors which they hadn't earned; the world was full of them; thus she tried to soothe her conscience. But she averted her eyes every time she passed the Buffalo Robe hanging over the fireplace in Mateka.

Slumber came hard to her that night, and when she finally did drop off it was to dream that the Buffalo Robe was being presented to her, but just as she put out her hand to take it Mary Sylvester appeared on the scene and called out loudly, "She doesn't deserve it!" and then all the girls pointed to her in scorn and repeated, "She doesn't deserve it!" "She doesn't deserve it!" until she ran away and hid herself in the woods.

So vivid was the dream that she wakened, trembling in ever limb, and burrowed into the pillow to shut out the sight of those dreadful pointing fingers, which still seemed to be before her eyes. Once awake she could not go back to sleep. She looked enviously across the tent at Hinpoha, who lay calm and peaceful in the moonlight, a faint smile parting her lips. She had nothing on her mind to keep her awake. Sahwah, too, was wrapped in profound slumber, her brow serene and untroubled; she had no uncomfortable secret to disturb her rest. How she envied them!

She envied Oh-Pshaw, who had taken the swimming test that day after a whole summer of trying to learn to swim, and was so proud of herself that she seemed to have grown an inch in height. There was no flaw in her happiness; she had won her honor fairly.

Then, as Agony lay there, her favorite heroines of history and fiction seemed to rise up and repudiate her - Robert Louis Stevenson, with whom she had formed an imaginary comradeship; there he stood looking at her scornfully and coldly; Joan of Arc, her especial heroine; she turned away in disgust; so all the others; one by one they reproached her.

Agony tossed for a long while and then rose, slipped on her bathrobe and shoes and stockings and wandered about for awhile, finally sitting down on a rustic bench on the veranda of Mateka, where she could look out on the river and the wide sky. Even the beauty of the night seemed to mock her. The big, bright stars, which used to twinkle in such a friendly fashion, now gleamed coldly at her; the light breeze rustling in the leaves was like so many spiteful whispers telling her secret. She had plucked a red lily that grew outside her tent door as she came out, and sat twirling it in her fingers. In an incredibly short time it whithered and let its petals droop. Agony gazed at it superstitiously. An old nurse had once told her that a flower would wither in the hand of a person who had told a lie. The idle tale came back to her now. Was it perhaps true after all? Did she have a withering touch now?

The things Miss Amesbury had said to her at sunset on the river the day before came back with startling force. "We carry our destiny in our own hands. We are what we make ourselves. Whatever kind of bud we are, just such a flower we will be. You are setting your face now in the direction in which you are going to travel. To be a noble woman you must have been a noble girl. The Future is only a great many Nows added up.

Every worthy action you perform now will make it easier to perform another one later on, and every unworthy one will do the same thing. If your lamp is dim you can't light the way for others...."

Agony looked at herself pitilessly and shuddered. Was this the road she was going to travel; was this the direction in which she had set her face? Cheat, deceiver, that was what she was. The winds whispered it; the river babbled it; the very stars seemed to twinkle it. Agony closed her eyes, and put her hands over her ears to shut out the little insinuating sounds; and in the silence her very heart beats throbbed it, rhythmically, pitilessly.

*   *   *   *   *

In the hour before dawn Miss Amesbury sat up in bed, under the impression that someone had called her name. Yes, there was someone on her balcony; in the dim light she could make out a drooping figure beside her bed.

"Miss Amesbury," faltered a low, but familiar voice.

"Why Agony, child!" exclaimed Miss Amesbury, now well awake and recognizing her visitor. "What is the matter? Are you sick?"

"Yes," replied Agony quietly, "sick of deceiving people."

And there, in the dim light, she told her whole story, the story of vaulting ambition and timely temptation, of action in haste and repentance at weary leisure.

"So that was it," Miss Amesbury exclaimed involuntarily, as Agony finished. "It seemed to me that you had something on your mnd; it puzzled me a great deal. How you must have suffered in conscience, poor child!"

She put out her hand and drew Agony down on the bed,

laying cool fingers on her hot forehead. Agony, entirely taken aback by Miss Amesbury's sympathetic attitude, for she had expected nothing but scorn and contempt, broke down and began to weep wildly. Miss Amesbury let her cry for awhile for she knew that the overburdened heart and strained nerves must find relief first of all. After awhile she began to speak soothing words, and gradually Agony's tempestuous sobs ceased and she grew calm. Then the two talked together for a long while, of the dangers of ambition, the seeking for personal glory at whatever cost. When the rising sun began to redden the ripples on the river Agony's heart once more knew peace, and she lay sleeping quietly, worn out, but tranquil in conscience. She had at last found the courage to make her decision; she would tell the Camp at Morning Sing the true story of the robin, and decline the honor of the Buffalo Robe. Agony's torch, dim and smoky for so long, at last was burning bright and high.

* * * * *

It was over. Agony sat on the deck of the *Carribou* beside Miss Amesbury. Camp had vanished from sight several minutes before behind an abrupt bend in the river, and was now only a memory. Agony sat pensive, her mind going back over the events of the day. It had been harder than she thought - to stand up in Mateka, and looking into the faces about her, tell the story of her deceit, but she had done it without flinching. Of course it had created a sensation. There was a painful silence, then several audible gasps of astonishment, and nervous giggles from the younger girls, and above these the scornful, unpleasant laugh of Jane Pratt. But Agony was strangely serene. Being prepared for almost any demonstration of scorn she was surprised that it was no worse. Now that the weight of deceit was off her conscience and the haunting fear of discovery put at an end the relief was so great that nothing else mattered. She bore it all tranquilly - Dr. Grayson's fatherly advice on the evils of ambition; the snubs of certain girls; Oh-Pshaw's sympathetic tears; Jo Severance's unforgettable look of unbelieving astonishment; Bengal Virden's prompt transferring of her affections to Sahwah; the loving loyalty of the Winnebagos, who said never a word of reproach.

And now it was all over, and she was going away with Miss Amesbury to spend a week with her in her home, going away the day before Camp closed. Miss Amesbury, loving friend that she was, realized that it was well both for Agony and for the rest of the girls that she should not be present at that farewell banquet where she was to have been presented with the Buffalo Robe, and had borne her away as soon as possible.

And now once more it was sunset, and the evening star was shining in the west, and it seemed to Agony that it had never seemed so fair and friendly before. Agony's face was pensive, but her heart was light, for now at last she knew that she was not a coward, and that "when the time came she would be able to do the brave and splendid thing."

Hildegard G. Frey

Choose from Thousands of 1stWorldLibrary Classics By

A. M. Barnard
Ada Leverson
Adolphus William Ward
Aesop
Agatha Christie
Alexander Aaronsohn
Alexander Kielland
Alexandre Dumas
Alfred Gatty
Alfred Ollivant
Alice Duer Miller
Alice Turner Curtis
Alice Dunbar
Ambrose Bierce
Amelia E. Barr
Amory H. Bradford
Andrew Lang
Andrew McFarland Davis
Andy Adams
Anna Sewell
Annie Besant
Annie Hamilton Donnell
Annie Payson Call
Annonaymous
Anton Chekhov
Arnold Bennett
Arthur Conan Doyle
Arthur M. Winfield
Arthur Ransome
Atticus
B.H. Baden-Powell
B. M. Bower
Baroness Emmuska Orczy
Baroness Orczy
Basil King
Bayard Taylor
Ben Macomber
Bertha Muzzy Bower
Bjornstjerne Bjornson
Booth Tarkington
Boyd Cable
Bram Stoker
C. Collodi
C. E. Orr
C. M. Ingleby
Carolyn Wells
Catherine Parr Traill
Charles A. Eastman
Charles Dickens

Charles Dudley Warner
Charles Farrar Browne
Charles Ives
Charles Kingsley
Charles Klein
Charles Amory Beach
Charles Hanson Towne
Charles Lathrop Pack
Charles Whibley
Charles Willing Beale
Charlotte M. Braeme
Charlotte M. Yonge
Charlotte Perkins Stetson
Clair W. Hayes
Clarence Day Jr.
Clarence E. Mulford
Clemence Housman
Confucius
Cornelis DeWitt Wilcox
Cyril Burleigh
D. H. Lawrence
Daniel Defoe
David Garnett
Dinah Craik
Don Carlos Janes
Donald Keyhoe
Dorothy Kilner
Dougan Clark
Douglas Fairbanks
E. Nesbit
E.P.Roe
E. Phillips Oppenheim
Earl Barnes
Edgar Rice Burroughs
Edith Van Dyne
Edith Wharton
Edward J. O'Biren
Edward S. Ellis
Edwin L. Arnold
Eleanor Atkins
Eliot Gregory
Elizabeth Gaskell
Elizabeth McCracken
Elizabeth Von Arnim
Ellem Key
Emerson Hough
Emilie F. Carlen
Emily Dickinson
Enid Bagnold

Enilor Macartney Lane
Erasmus W. Jones
Ernie Howard Pie
Ethel Turner
Ethel Watts Mumford
Eugenie Foa
Eugene Wood
Eustace Hale Ball
Evelyn Everett-green
Everard Cotes
F. H. Cheley
F. J. Cross
Federick Austin Ogg
Ferdinand Ossendowski
Francis Bacon
Francis Darwin
Frances Hodgson Burnett
Frances Parkinson Keyes
Frank Gee Patchin
Frank Harris
Frank Jewett Mather
Frank L. Packard
Frank V. Webster
Frederic Stewart Isham
Frederick Trevor Hill
Frederick Winslow Taylor
Friedrich Kerst
Friedrich Nietzsche
Fyodor Dostoyevsky
G.A. Henty
G.K. Chesterton
Gabrielle E. Jackson
Garrett P. Serviss
Gaston Leroux
George A. Warren
George Ade
Geroge Bernard Shaw
George Durston
George Ebers
George Eliot
George Gissing
George MacDonald
George Meredith
George Orwell
George Sylvester Viereck
George Tucker
George W. Cable
George Wharton James
Gertrude Atherton

Grace E. King
Grace Gallatin
Grant Allen
Guillermo A. Sherwell
Gulielma Zollinger
Gustav Flaubert
H. A. Cody
H. B. Irving
H.C. Bailey
H. G. Wells
H. H. Munro
H. Irving Hancock
H. Rider Haggard
H. W. C. Davis
Hamilton Wright Mabie
Hans Christian Andersen
Harold Avery
Harold McGrath
Harriet Beecher Stowe
Harry Houidini
Helent Hunt Jackson
Helen Nicolay
Hendrik Conscience
Hendy David Thoreau
Henri Barbusse
Henrik Ibsen
Henry Adams
Henry Ford
Henry Frost
Henry James
Henry Jones Ford
Henry Seton Merriman
Henry W Longfellow
Herbert A. Giles
Herbert N. Casson
Herman Hesse
Homer
Honore De Balzac
Horace Walpole
Horatio Alger Jr.
Howard Pyle
Howard R. Garis
Hugh Lofting
Hugh Walpole
Humphry Ward
Ian Maclaren
Inez Haynes Gillmore
Irving Bacheller
Israel Abrahams
Ivan Turgenev
J.G.Austin

J. Henri Fabre
J. M. Barrie
J. Macdonald Oxley
J. S. Fletcher
J. S. Knowles
J. Storer Clouston
Jack London
Jacob Abbott
James Allen
James Andrews
James Baldwin
James DeMille
James Joyce
James Lane Allen
James Lane Allen
James Oliver Curwood
James Oppenheim
James Otis
James R. Driscoll
Jane Austen
Janet Aldridge
Jens Peter Jacobsen
Jerome K. Jerome
John Burroughs
John Cournos
John F. Kennedy
John Gay
John Glasworthy
John Habberton
John Joy Bell
John Kendrick Bangs
John Milton
John Philip Sousa
Jonas Lauritz Idemil Lie
Jonathan Swift
Joseph A. Altsheler
Joseph Carey
Joseph Conrad
Joseph E. Badger Jr
Joseph Hergesheimer
Joseph Jacobs
Jules Vernes
Julian Hawthrone
Julie A Lippmann
Justin Huntly McCarthy
Kakuzo Okakura
Kenneth Grahame
Kenneth McGaffey
Kate Langley Bosher
Kate Langley Bosher
Katherine Cecil Thurston

Katherine Stokes
L. A. Abbot
L. T. Meade
L. Frank Baum
Latta Griswold
Laura Lee Hope
Laurence Housman
Lawrence Beasley
Leo Tolstoy
Leonid Andreyev
Lewis Carroll
Lewis Sperry Chafer
Lilian Bell
Lloyd Osbourne
Louis Hughes
Louis Tracy
Louisa May Alcott
Lucy Fitch Perkins
Lucy Maud Montgomery
Lydia Miller Middleton
Lyndon Orr
M. Corvus
M. H. Adams
Margaret E. Sangster
Margaret Vandercook
Margret Penrose
Maria Edgeworth
Maria Thompson Daviess
Mariano Azuela
Marion Polk Angellotti
Mark Overton
Mark Twain
Mary Austin
Mary Catherine Crowley
Mary Cole
Mary Hastings Bradley
Mary Roberts Rinehart
Mary Rowlandson
M. Wollstonecraft Shelley
Maud Lindsay
Max Beerbohm
Myra Kelly
Nathaniel Hawthrone
Nicolo Machiavelli
O. F. Walton
Oscar Wilde
Owen Johnson
P.G. Wodehouse
Paul and Mabel Thorne
Paul G. Tomlinson
Paul Severing

Percy Brebner
Peter B. Kyne
Plato
R. Derby Holmes
R. L. Stevenson
R. S. Ball
Rabindranath Tagore
Rahul Alvares
Ralph Bonehill
Ralph Henry Barbour
Ralph Victor
Ralph Waldo Emmerson
Rene Descartes
Rex Beach
Rex E. Beach
Richard Harding Davis
Richard Jefferies
Richard Le Gallienne
Robert Barr
Robert Frost
Robert Gordon Anderson
Robert L. Drake
Robert Lansing
Robert Lynd
Robert Michael Ballantyne
Robert W. Chambers
Rosa Nouchette Carey
Rudyard Kipling
Samuel B. Allison

Samuel Hopkins Adams
Sarah Bernhardt
Sarah C. Hallowell
Selma Lagerlof
Sherwood Anderson
Sigmund Freud
Standish O'Grady
Stanley Weyman
Stella Benson
Stephen Crane
Stewart Edward White
Stijn Streuvels
Swami Abhedananda
Swami Parmananda
T. S. Ackland
T. S. Arthur
The Princess Der Ling
Thomas A. Janvier
Thomas A Kempis
Thomas Anderton
Thomas Bailey Aldrich
Thomas Bulfinch
Thomas De Quincey
Thomas H. Huxley
Thomas Hardy
Thomas More
Thornton W. Burgess
U. S. Grant
Valentine Williams

Various Authors
Vaughan Kester
Victor Appleton
Virginia Woolf
Walter Camp
Walter Scott
Washington Irving
Wilbur Lawton
Wilkie Collins
Willa Cather
Willard F. Baker
William Dean Howells
William le Queux
W. Makepeace Thackeray
William W. Walter
Winston Churchill
Yei Theodora Ozaki
Yogi Ramacharaka
Young E. Allison
Zane Grey